PUFFIN BOOKS

THE GHOSTLY TERM AT TREBIZON

Ghosts are the least of Rebecca's worries at the beginning of her year in the Fifth at Trebizon. After her success at the England Junior Grass Court Championships, the accident was a real setback – vital months of practice would be lost. Robbie had been driving them back to Trebizon when he had to brake hard to avoid a deer and Rebecca was thrown forward, breaking her wrist.

Of course, Robbie blamed himself and thought Rebecca blamed him too! Upset by the strain in their friendship and worried about her GCSE maths coursework, Rebecca is delighted when she meets Cliff, an old school friend from London. But after Cliff has taken her to a disco, she is frightened by the sight of a ghostly figure in Trebizon's grounds and the sounds of an intruder in Court House.

Rebecca, Tish, Sue and the others refuse to believe the stories of the Court House ghost, but who or what could be behind these strange events? Suspense and intrigue brew up to a fitting climax in this the eleventh book in the terrific Trebizon series.

Anne Digby was born in Kingston upon Thames, Surrey but lived in the west country for many years. As well as the Trebizon books, she is the author of the popular *Me, Jill Robinson* series.

ANNE DIGBY

THE GHOSTLY TERM AT
TREBIZON

PUFFIN BOOKS

PUFFIN BOOKS

Published by the Penguin Group
27 Wrights Lane, London w8 5 tz, England
Viking Penguin Inc., 40 West 23rd Street, New York, New York 10010, USA
Penguin Books Australia Ltd, Ringwood, Victoria, Australia
Penguin Books Canada Ltd, 2801 John Street, Markham, Ontario, Canada L3R 1B4
Penguin Books (NZ) Ltd, 182–190 Wairau Road, Auckland 10, New Zealand

Penguin Books Ltd, Registered Offices: Harmondsworth, Middlesex, England

First published 1990
10 9 8 7 6 5 4 3 2 1

Made and printed in Great Britain by
Cox and Wyman Ltd, Reading, Berks.
Filmset in Linotron Ehrhardt by
Rowland Phototypesetting Ltd, Bury St Edmunds, Suffolk

CONTENTS

ONE

WAITING FOR REBECCA

When Rebecca Mason moved into the top floor of Court House, it didn't strike her as being the least bit ghostly. She arrived back at school, to start life as a Fifth Year, on a golden September evening. The sun's rays slanted in through the little attic window of the cubicle her friends had saved for her. It looked warm and cosy in there: a bed, her own desk and chair; a brown woolly rug on the shiny waxed and polished floorboards; a fitted cupboard in the corner to hang her clothes in.

No ghosts here. There was no reason why there should be. Everyone knew that the ghost story that last year's Fifths had made up, about a jilted Victorian schoolmaster and his ghostly cat, had been a huge practical joke from start to finish. They'd been simply laying the ground for the house Christmas party, when the lights had suddenly gone out and Sarah Turner had burst in. Wearing Moyra Milton's luminous face paints and Mr Barrington's old university gown and mortar board – and carrying a cat!

It hadn't frightened anyone – not even Mara. As for the cat, the Fifths had borrowed the ginger and white from the Douglases in Norris House. Moggy, apart from being fat and sleepy and fluffy (and quite wrong for a ghostly role), was recognized at once, amidst hoots of laughter.

Rebecca smiled at the memory. It wasn't the thought of a Victorian ghost that had ruined her day. It was something much more solid than that.

'That's all the luggage up from the car,' said her father. 'Nice window you've got. A skylight, too. Your own partitioned room, your own desk. You'll be able to get your head down for that GCSE now, won't you?'

'That's about all I will be able to do,' said Rebecca bitterly.

'Cheer up, Becky,' said her mother. 'Shall we put these posters up for you –?'

'It's all right, Mum. Tish or someone can help with all that. I must *dash* now, I'm hungry. I'll miss tea. They'll all be wondering what on earth's happened to me.'

Her parents looked anxious so Rebecca put on a cheerful face:

'Come on, Dad. I'll come down and see you both off. You've got a long drive back. You'll be tired out!'

'It's certainly been an eventful day,' agreed her father.

Oddly enough, the joke that last year's Fifths had invented about a Court House ghost came into Sue Murdoch's mind on the train. It was early on in the journey. She thought of it in the buffet car, seeing Roberta Jones in there trying to write another of her plays.

It was fun travelling to Trebizon by train.

With the sole exception of Rebecca, 'the six' were all coming back together on the school train this year. They met up at Paddington station and found an empty compartment where they could lounge around and talk and laugh and catch up on everything that had happened in the long summer holidays.

'And how is *Rebecca?*' Mara Leonodis asked Tish Anderson, who'd been at Rebecca's house that same morning. 'Oh, I wanted so much to come and see her play at Eastbourne but father kept me in Athens. She did brilliantly! And you did brilliantly in your race at Birmingham, Tish. I wanted to fly to England and see you both. It was horrible having to stay in Greece!'

'*Poor* Mara,' said Sue. 'Having to stay in sunny Greece when she could have been in glorious rain-sodden England.'

They all laughed. It had been a very wet August.

'Rebecca's in great form,' said Tish. 'I expect she'll be back at school before we are, if Robbie does much of the driving.'

Tish had only seen Rebecca for ten minutes while her father dropped off Robbie and all his luggage (and most of Tish's luggage) at the Masons' house in south London. That lot had headed off to the west country by car but with such a load on board there wasn't room for Tish herself, which was why she was on the train.

'How come Robbie hogged a place in Mr Mason's car instead of you, Tish?' asked Margot Lawrence. Robbie Anderson was at Garth College, which was very near Trebizon. They were due back today, too. Sue's brothers, David and Edward, went there as well and were somewhere up the train.

'To do some of the driving,' chipped in Sue.

'And I wish them luck!' grinned Tish. 'Robbie's been

like a shipwrecked sailor all holidays, ever since his car packed up. You should have seen him checking over Mr Mason's car the minute we got there! It's only an old hired Ford or something but apparently it *goes*. Wild horses wouldn't have stopped my brother getting in on the act!'

'Oh, Tish,' said Sue, glancing at her through her spectacles with a slightly schoolmistressy expression.

'Am I being unfair?' laughed Tish.

Rebecca had chatted to Sue on the phone about it.

'You know you are.'

'Don't let's talk about cars,' said Sally (Elf) Elphinstone. She'd noticed a lot of people passing down the train in the last few minutes. 'If we're going to the buffet car we'd better go. Or all the best drinks and crisps will have sold out.'

'Has Robbie's car conked out then?' asked Margot as they walked down the swaying train. 'That nice old car. After all the hard work he did on it!'

'What a shame,' said Mara.

They all managed to squeeze round one table in the buffet car, munched crisps, drank Coke and talked about going on to the top floor at Court House.

'It'll be lovely up there, won't it!' said Elf. 'Right up in the eaves, where all the maidservants used to live in the old days. And we'll each have our own cubie. Talk about gracious living.'

'I want the one nearest the fire escape,' announced Tish. 'There's a door out on to the balcony, and the fire escape leads down from that balcony. I can sneak out for early morning runs without waking the whole floor up.'

'You're welcome,' said Sue, pretending to shiver. 'According to Moyra it's nothing but draughts in that corner.'

'Tish never feels the cold,' smiled Margot.

Somebody came and settled down heavily at the table across the gangway. With a deep sigh she started scribbling into an exercise book, then sighed again and sat chewing her biro. It was Roberta Jones, a new Fifth Year like themselves but in Norris House.

'Catching up on some coursework?' asked Mara sympathetically.

'Good heavens, no, I'm writing the Christmas house play,' stated Roberta. She was the founder of a middle school drama group and also its mainstay, together with her best friend Deborah Rickard and the Nathan twins – Sarah and Ruth. They put on little shows in Norris House from time to time. 'But I'm not satisfied with Debbie's part. She's such a brilliant actress, isn't she, I've got to get it just right.'

'Why don't you write about the Court House ghost then?' Sue called across. 'Good wholesome Christmas entertainment.'

'Brilliant,' agreed Tish, who couldn't stand Debbie Rickard. 'Brilliant part for Debbie.'

'What ghost?' asked Roberta.

'The ghost of a Victorian schoolmaster who haunts the top floor of Court House!' explained Sue. 'Him and his cat. All because of unrequited love. Want a cheese and onion?' She passed the crisp bag.

'Who didn't requite his love?'

'Some maidservant. The most beautiful upstairs maid who ever lived, with a peaches and cream complexion,' said Sue, embellishing the story as she went along. 'She jilted him.'

'She said she preferred his cat to him,' interposed Tish. 'So he went and hanged himself from the rafters – right above the cubie where I'm going to be sleeping . . .'

'Oh, Tish, he didn't!' objected Mara. 'He ran away to sea, taking his cat with him.'

'Oh yes, that's right, I forgot,' apologized Tish. 'Went to sea – but put a curse on her. Said he and his cat would haunt the servants' quarters of Court House for ever more.'

'Hmmm, none of that fits in with the play I'm writing,' yawned Roberta. 'And Debbie wouldn't want to play a beautiful maidservant.'

'We could lend her a mask,' said Tish. 'Or how about the cat?'

'I know you're just trying to help,' said Roberta crossly, 'but would you mind shutting up? I've got to get this finished on the train. I promised Debbie I'd bring it back to school with me. She's dying to read it.'

'There's Curly!' squealed Mara, leaping to her feet. 'Look, the boys are on the train. I never knew!'

Soon the girls were talking to Curly Watson, Mike Brown and Chris Earl-Smith from Garth College, the ghost forgotten.

But the conversation with Roberta was going to have one small repercussion. When she went back to her carriage, she solemnly imparted the story of the Court House ghost to Alice Burridge and Katy Baxter, who were just starting in the Third Year at Trebizon. They'd spent their first two years in Juniper, the junior boarding house, and were now due to move into Court.

And at about four o'clock that afternoon, with their cubicles bagged and unpacking well under way, Tish and the others suddenly heard a funny wailing sound coming from the other side of the glass door that led to the fire escape.

'Whooooooo . . . Whoooo . . .'

They rushed out on to the balcony, just in time to see three figures disappearing down the fire escape, giggling noisily. Alice Burridge, Katy Baxter and Lizzy Douglas, who had been billeted in Court House to be independent of her parents, who ran Norris.

'Clear off, you stupid young idiots!' Tish hollered down. 'Or you'll get a bucket of water over your heads.'

'You're not allowed on this fire escape!' cried Elf.

'It is *our* fire escape and Third Years are *not allowed* on it,' shouted Margot.

The friends came back inside, slammed the door shut behind them, and leant against the wall laughing helplessly.

'I've been longing to say that for years!' said Elf gleefully. 'The times it's been said to us!'

'Isn't it just great being Fifth Years?' agreed Tish. 'Aren't we important.'

They explored their new quarters thoroughly and then made some hot chocolate in the little kitchen at the end.

'You were wrong about one thing, Tish,' said Mara. 'Rebecca hasn't got here first, after all.'

When the bell went for tea nearly two hours later, Rebecca still hadn't arrived.

'Whatever's happened to her?' said Sue to Tish, as they all walked across the school grounds to the dining hall in main building. 'She's really *late*.'

Tish shrugged. 'Maybe Robbie just couldn't bear to stop driving. Maybe they're at Land's End by now. Or maybe he's pranged the car.'

'Hope not,' said Sue drily. 'That wasn't the idea at all, was it?'

'Nope. *And* they've got my luggage.'

THE EMERGENCY

Rebecca loved having her parents back from Saudi Arabia on summer leave. She loved being at home again, the terraced house in south London that was let out for the rest of the year. It was fun meeting up with Claire and Amanda, her old friends from comprehensive school, going to a disco with them and catching up on local news. Cliff Haynes had moved to the west country apparently – somewhere near Trebizon!

Of course, the high spot of the summer holidays was Eastbourne – the England Junior Grass Court Championships. Getting accepted for the national event was a new high in Rebecca's remarkable tennis career. It had been tough, battling her way up the computer rankings – but she'd made it.

Her father had booked the hotel just as soon as Rebecca's acceptance arrived.

'Your mother and I like Eastbourne. It'll be a nice little holiday for us while you're enjoying yourself playing tennis.'

Rebecca had simply been amused at that stage to

realize that her parents were so out of touch. She wasn't going to Eastbourne to enjoy herself! She had to try and make her mark on the national scene. This was her big chance! She looked forward to it with a tight little feeling in the throat, a mixture of excitement and apprehension. How would she get on? Would she, after all the hassle to get there, simply find herself knocked out in the first round?

However, long before Eastbourne, as her parents drove her to a minor tournament here, a coaching session there, it began to dawn on Rebecca that Mum and Dad were even more clueless than she'd realized. They had no inkling of how high-powered the junior game was these days! How competitive! How much everyone had to put into it, family included.

'I don't know how some of these parents find the time,' her father had said to her in genuine bewilderment, after they'd arrived back at two in the morning from a 16U competition in Wales. ('It'll warm you up nicely for Eastbourne,' Rebecca's coach had told her. 'You must go.')

Another time, starting to knock a ball against the wall at home, after a long practice session at the local club, Mrs Mason had called her into supper and said, in exasperation:

'Rebecca, don't you think that's enough for one day?'

'What about doing some GCSE coursework?' her father said as they ate their supper. 'Miss Welbeck made a point of that.'

'Why can't I see my report?' asked Rebecca. Her parents had been to visit Trebizon's principal at the end of the summer term and had been secretive ever since.

'We'll show you some time,' said her mother evasively. 'We had no idea this tennis took up so much of your time.'

'And ours!' smiled her father.

It was after Eastbourne that things came to a head.

It was one of the wettest tournaments ever, rain stopping play, matches postponed. But Rebecca had a marvellous tournament!

She reached the quarter-finals and even then was only narrowly beaten.

'I almost reached the *semi-finals*!' she sighed, as they drove back to London. She was glowing with exhilaration; it had been a thrilling few days. 'If only I had! Then I could have played Rachel Cathcart. We're neck and neck on the computer. We always seem to be. And I've never played her.'

'There's time yet,' said her mother.

Rebecca nodded. They were bound to meet up in the next twelve months. Somewhere. She and Rachel Cathcart. Rebecca intended to get better and better, to go on improving . . .

'We're very proud of you, Becky,' said her father and meant it.

The following day was wet again and Rebecca said:

'Well, at least you haven't got to hang around in the rain today! Lucky I got knocked out, wasn't it!'

It was only a joke, but it caught Mrs Mason off guard.

'It was a bit miserable, wasn't it. We didn't get to the beach once.'

She looked so wistful. Suddenly, guiltily, Rebecca realized it hadn't been much of a little holiday for them after all. But there was more to it than that – and the crunch came that afternoon.

'Mum! Dad! Tish just phoned. It's her big race in Birmingham tomorrow. Can I go and stay with them tonight? Dr Anderson says he'll take us all up in the car tomorrow – so we can watch the race. Can I go to the Andersons? Can you take me?'

'No, I can't!' exploded Mr Mason. 'We've already got one sports star in the family, isn't that enough? I'm supposed to be on holiday!'

'Your father wants to watch the snooker,' scolded Mrs Mason.

Rebecca disappeared off to her room, feeling tearful. Dad suddenly snapping at her like that had come as a nasty surprise. She wanted time to think about it. She sat on her bed and thought about it carefully.

Then her mother came in and put an arm round her shoulders.

'He didn't mean to be angry. But we seem to have been driving all holidays. Hertfordshire's right the other side of London, you know how Daddy hates the M25. The roads are so crowded in England now! Daddy needs a rest. He needs this holiday. He's not as young as he was.'

'It was stupid of me to ask,' said Rebecca. 'I've been really selfish. I've been taking you both for granted. I can just as easily get a coach from Victoria – I'm sure the Andersons can meet me. Robbie's car's packed up but one of them will meet me.'

So Rebecca went to Hertfordshire and on to Birmingham, watched Tish come third in the 1500 metres and thoroughly enjoyed herself. But she told Tish about the little family squabble.

'I feel so mean. I just didn't think. I should have realized that Dad was getting tired. He works pretty hard out there and it's hot as well. I just imagined everyone liked driving.'

Tish in turn confided this to Robbie.

So when the time came for Mr and Mrs Mason to drive Rebecca back to school, before departing for Saudi Arabia once more, it was only natural that Robbie stepped in.

He'd love the chance to do some driving again, he humbly suggested to Mr Mason. Could he travel back to school with them, please?

Mr Mason maneouvred the car out of London then drove as far as the Fleet service station on the M3. They stopped for coffee. Rebecca bought some barley sugars in the shop. Then back to the car and Robbie and her father changed places.

'Right, let's see how you go, my lad.'

Mr Mason had no need to worry. Tish's brother was a young driver but a good one, courteous to other road users, totally alert. He also had excellent reflexes, which was just as well as things turned out.

As they cruised along the motorway and then took the A303 to the west country, everybody was very relaxed. The sun shining, the countryside sailing by, the view breathtaking as they went over Salisbury Plain. Rebecca's father chatted amiably to Robbie in the front, while Rebecca and her mother sat in the back, making the most of this time together.

'There's Stonehenge!' exclaimed Mr Mason, craning his head round as it passed to their right. 'How nice not to be driving. I can get a proper look at it.'

'Oh, I've missed it,' said Robbie, whose eyes had been

trained on the road ahead. By the time he glanced sidelong, it had gone. Never mind, he thought, nice little bus this one.

'Robbie, have a barley sugar,' said Rebecca, leaning forward and carefully popping one into his mouth. 'OK?'

'Don't forget to video that programme, will you, Becky? The Trebizon film. I don't trust Granny. When did you say it's going to be on?'

'I didn't, Mum.' *Trebizon Observed*, a documentary film about life at the school last term, included four of the games when Rebecca won the county closed tennis championship. 'The date isn't fixed yet. We'll be told in advance though.'

'Well, your grandmother's all prepared,' chuckled Mr Mason. He'd bought his mother a video recorder on this trip. They'd taken it up to Gloucestershire and with much patience instructed her in its use.

'Oh, we'll record it at school, all right,' said Rebecca.

'I'll tape it as well,' volunteered Robbie.

'Then Daddy and I can watch it when we come home next summer!' sighed Mrs Mason. 'And I wonder how much further you'll have got with your tennis by then, Becky?'

'A lot further, I hope, Mum.'

After a picnic lunch, Robbie asked if he could carry on driving. 'After all, you've got the long haul back, sir.'

'With pleasure, son,' said Mr Mason.

And without doubt Robbie was driving beautifully.

The emergency, when it came, was possibly not his fault. Few people could have foreseen it.

They were almost there.

Bowling along the leafy lane that led to Garth College.

As the college gates came in sight, Rebecca in the rear released her seat belt. It would be nice to get out and stretch her legs while Robbie unloaded his luggage. Give him a hug goodbye. Then, on to Trebizon . . .

It came from nowhere.

Spindly legs, huge startled eyes, soaring through the air from behind a hedge. For a moment Rebecca thought the deer was going to land on top of the car.

'Watch out!' yelled Robbie in warning as he stamped violently on the brake pedal. EEEEEEEEEEEE.

Rebecca was flung forward with tremendous force, the palm of her left hand taking all the impact as it hit the seat in front. There was a horrible jarring sensation in her wrist; she felt something go. But there was no pain.

The deer stood perplexed in the middle of the road facing them, right in front of the car's bonnet. It stared wild-eyed through the windscreen at them, then fled.

'Phew,' said Robbie.

'Well done, son,' said Mr Mason in admiration.

'Are you all right, Becky?' asked her mother, in the back. 'What happened to your seat belt?'

'It's all right, Mum, I'm fine,' Rebecca said quickly.

They were all a bit shaken. They just sat there for a few moments. Then slowly, calmly, Robbie took the car on down the lane, in through the gates of Garth College and across to Syon House, his boarding house.

Mr Mason got out and helped Robbie unload his luggage. For some reason Rebecca didn't feel like getting out any more. Robbie ducked his head in to say goodbye. 'I'll see you soon, Rebeck. You all right? You look a bit pale.'

'I'm fine,' smiled Rebecca, though actually she felt as

though she were going to be sick. 'Thanks for coming down with us, see you.'

With shouts of 'See you next year, Robbie!' and 'Good luck with Oxford!' her father turned the car round and they drove off.

'Nearly at Trebizon,' said Mrs Mason, glancing at Rebecca anxiously. 'Look, here's the town.'

They were passing the 30 m.p.h. speed-restriction signs on the outskirts of the town of Trebizon. The school lay above the town on the other side. But Rebecca wasn't looking. She was staring down at her left wrist, touching it gingerly.

'There's something wrong, Mum. It feels funny.'

Her father stopped the car while her mother examined the wrist.

'I think it's broken, Becky,' she said in great concern.

They took her straight to the out-patients department of St Michael's, the pleasant small hospital in the centre of the town. There were long waits while X-rays were taken and doctors consulted.

When they left, Rebecca's left forearm was encased in plaster and she had been booked in for future visits. It was a rather complicated injury but with the right care and regular physiotherapy the wrist would be as good as new again by Christmas at the latest.

Christmas! Rebecca was horrified.

'I'm right-handed so I *can* play some tennis –?' she blurted out. 'When the plaster's off?'

'Certainly not,' said the doctor. 'No racket sports. You're not to throw things or lift things with that left hand – and that includes tennis balls. Not until I say you can.'

Rebecca felt very tearful as they drove to school.

But now the time had come to say goodbye to her parents, she put a brave face on things. They had seen Mrs Barrington and taken up all the luggage and now, back down at the car, they parted company.

'I'm going to be fine,' insisted Rebecca. 'It's a nice little hospital, isn't it? I'm so hungry! I mustn't miss tea!'

Her father kissed her on the cheek, took one last look at the arm in plaster and said: 'It's rotten luck, Becky, it really is. But there's always a reason for things, that's what I've found. The bigger the disappointment, the more it can turn out to be for the best.'

Rebecca waved the car out of sight, smiled bravely, and wondered what on earth her father was talking about.

THREE

A BARRIER

'Rebecca! Where have you *been*?' cried Mara, catching a glimpse of her pale face as she threaded her way through the crowded dining hall to the place they'd saved for her. Dozens of heads were turning at her late arrival. What had Rebecca Mason done to her arm, for goodness' sake? Why was it in plaster? Why was she wearing a sling?

'Thank goodness you're all right,' said Sue, as Rebecca sat down. Her eyes were fixed on Rebecca's arm. 'Well, *almost* all right.'

'What's happened?' they all demanded. They were looking at Rebecca's plaster cast in horror, especially Tish.

'Did Robbie crash the car?' she asked palely.

'No he did *not*,' said Rebecca instantly. 'He was brilliant. It was my fault – I'd taken my seat belt off.'

She told them all about it, then had to repeat the story several times as people came up to her on their way out of dining hall. Tea had finished now.

'I'm trying to eat my jacket potato!' Rebecca finally snapped at the Nathan twins as they approached her with

Roberta Jones. 'I'm *starving.*' Thank goodness the others had saved her plenty of food.

'We were only asking,' said Sarah and Ruth in unison.

'Did you finish the play, Bert?' asked Elf. 'Did Debbie like it?'

In reply she got the biggest scowl from Roberta Jones that Rebecca had ever seen.

'What's eating Robert?' she inquired as the threesome went off.

'Maybe Debbie didn't like the play,' suggested Margot.

'Perhaps the part wasn't just quite brilliant enough for her,' commented Tish acidly.

'Where is Debbie Rickard anyway?' inquired Elf. 'I haven't seen her.'

'Do you think Robert's just seen the Court House ghost?' giggled Sue. And they told Rebecca all about the conversation on the train and how the word had spread and the new Thirds had already latched on to it.

'It's going to be fun having the fire escape,' commented Rebecca.

It was nice the way they all waited for her to finish her tea and then took her back to Court House in a jostling, chattering group. Nothing seemed quite so bad now she was surrounded by her friends, so protective, so sympathetic about what had happened.

Up on the top floor, while Tish did her own unpacking, the other four emptied Rebecca's cases, arranged things neatly in drawers, asked her exactly how she wanted her posters put up. It was really rather luxurious being an invalid; being spoiled. She wandered around and explored the top floor.

'I like your cubie, Jenny,' she said to Jenny Brook-Hayes. 'Lovely view.' She gazed through the dormer window across to the roof tops of main school: the lovely old manor house that formed its heart, the modern science block, the converted coach house with its clock tower. 'You always like being at the front.'

Rebecca on the other hand preferred being at the back. It was very peaceful there, overlooking the garden. And beyond the garden the back of Norris House, which had been converted from what were once the stables and outbuildings of Court House. She was pleased with the cubicle the others had saved her. Tish was in the corner cubicle, next to a spacious area with a large table and a couple of power points for kettles and so forth. This area was in front of the big glass door that led to the balcony and the fire escape. Rebecca's cubicle was to the right of that open space, its left-hand partition wall hard up against the table.

'I'll be able to nip out of my cubie and round the corner in the mornings and make myself a cup of tea!' she'd exclaimed. 'Then sun myself on the balcony in my dressing-gown.'

'And I'll join you!' Tish had said in glee.

Rebecca wandered back there now, attracted by the large crowd gathered round the big table. Everyone was laughing and exclaiming.

'Rebecca – come and see what Mara's brought back!' yelled Elf.

The crowd parted to let Rebecca through, careful of her bad arm.

Something had been placed on the table and Tish was

plugging it in. It was a superb little photocopier, really dinky! Trust Mara to have some exciting loot.

'Let's see if it works,' Fiona Freeman was saying eagerly.

'Here, I've got something I wanted copied,' said Aba Amori. The Nigerian girl produced a magazine cutting. 'I've got to give this back to Laura Wilkins but it's really useful. It's full of stuff I need for my geography course-work.'

'Can I have one?' cried Margot.

'Mara, it's fantastic,' said Rebecca, as Tish fed some paper in and fiddled with the controls. 'Where did you get it?'

'I told Papa we needed one to help us pass our GCSE,' laughed Mara, her brown eyes shining. 'He believed me!'

Swish. Almost silently the small machine produced two perfect copies of Aba's magazine cutting. Cheers went up.

'Brilliant, Mara!' exclaimed Ann Ferguson.

'It'll be really useful,' nodded Anne Finch.

'It'll save us having to go over to the office when we want to get things copied,' said Rebecca in delight.

She was feeling almost cheerful again. But at hot-chocolate time, sitting on her bed and wondering how long it was going to take to get ready for bed with only one usable arm, the dark cloud of what had happened settled back over her head.

Tish came in and sat beside her.

'It's filthy luck, isn't it, Rebeck. How's Robbie taken it?'

'He doesn't even know yet,' replied Rebecca in a dull voice.

'*Whaa-ttt?*'

'Well, Dad dropped him off at Garth and it was only after –'

But Tish had leapt up and was half-way out of the cubicle.

'Robbie doesn't even know? That's awful. He ought to know! Come on, Rebeck. Quick. Let's phone him.'

'Oh Tish, I'm tired –' protested Rebecca. To the empty air.

Sighing, she padded her way along the length of the floor, between the main rows of cubicles, then out through the far doors and down the stairs. All the way down to the payphone on the ground floor.

Tish had already got through –

'That emergency stop you did, Robbie.'

'What about it? Rather a beauty though I say so myself. What's all this about, Tish? I'm just off to bed.'

The thought of Robbie having a nice evening while the rest of them had been worrying about Rebecca suddenly provoked Tish's temper.

'Such a beauty that Rebeck's smashed her wrist up! She can't play tennis – not properly – she can't play again till Christmas.'

'*WHAT?*' Robbie was stunned.

Rebecca snatched the phone from Tish.

'Robbie –'

'Is this *true*, Rebeck?'

'Yes.' Rebecca explained everything while Robbie listened in shocked silence.

'I should have been going slower,' he said hoarsely, finding his voice at last. 'I should have thought about the deer there –'

'Oh, Robbie, don't be silly. It was entirely *my own fault*. I'd slipped out of my seat belt, remember, thinking we were almost there. It was *my* fault.'

'I've got to come and see you, Rebeck!' was Robbie's main concern. 'The first minute I can.'

They arranged that he'd cycle over on Saturday morning.

Before Rebecca rang off, Tish grabbed the phone back.

'Sorry, Robbie. I just felt like shouting at someone. I don't suppose it was your fault really.'

'Night, Tish,' he said wearily. 'It probably was. I just don't know.'

The next day, Friday, had its ups and downs for Rebecca.

The new Fifth Year timetables were given out. There'd been a bit of a shake-up of the three maths divisions. Rebecca had always been in Division 1 with the others but now found herself placed in Division 2. At least she had Mara to keep her company. In her heart she'd expected it, after failing maths in the school's summer exams.

All the girls in Division 1 would be taking the top paper in GCSE next summer and were expected to get either A or B grades. Their lessons were going to move at a brisk pace in the Fifth, with some of them – like Tish Anderson and Josselyn Vining – being prepared for an extra paper. The pace in Div 2 would be less alarming, explained Miss Hort, who would be teaching them.

'Does that mean Mara and I can't take the top paper next summer?' Rebecca asked in dismay. She'd resolved to work hard this year – to slog and slog. Now this! 'Does that mean we won't be allowed to carry on with the top-level coursework any more? But then I can't get any higher than a C grade. No matter how hard I try –'

'Means nothing of the sort,' replied Miss Hort brusquely. 'If that were the case we'd have placed you and Mara in Division 3.'

Div 3, thought Rebecca, with Roberta Jones and Susan McTavish and Jane O'Hara and that lot.

'In Div 2 we do at least cover all the work required for the top paper,' continued Miss Hort. 'You *may* be allowed to continue with the advanced coursework. You *may* even be allowed to take the top paper. On the other hand you may not. It will depend entirely on your progress.'

'You mean I'm in with a chance?' asked Rebecca in relief.

'Chance doesn't come into it,' said the mannish Miss Hort. But the eyes were twinkling behind the horn-rimmed spectacles. 'Effort, not chance, comes into it.'

It was a salutary experience.

It was also rather annoying when Mr Oppenheimer compared Rebecca's cross-section diagram of a plant unfavourably with Debbie Rickard's in biology.

'Scrappy, Rebecca. You usually do better than this. Deborah's here is an absolute model.' He held it up and showed the class. 'Perfect clarity. Meticulous labelling.'

Rebecca looked at it in surprise. Debbie's work was usually OK but this effort, certainly, was rather outstanding.

'You must put this by for your practical file, Deborah,' said the biology teacher, handing it back. 'The examiners will like this.'

Roberta Jones, who was rather good at biology herself, looked discontented.

'Why aren't Robert and Debbie sitting together?' whispered Rebecca.

'Haven't you heard? They've fallen out!' hissed Elf. 'Debbie's not boarding any more. Her parents have bought a house in Trebizon and she's changed to day. Bert's furious!'

'Debbie doesn't want to be in Robert's house play. She says she can't keep fagging back to school in the evenings for rehearsals and so on,' chipped in Margot. 'So the Nathan twins don't want to be in it either and the whole thing's been scrapped.'

'Oh!' whispered Rebecca, in enlightenment. So that had been the reason for Roberta's great scowl the previous day.

'What's the betting Debbie's Dad did that diagram for her?' commented Tish with a grin, before being told to stop whispering.

While the rest of the Fifths played hockey and netball that afternoon, things looked up slightly for Rebecca. Mrs Ericson, her tennis coach, drove over especially to see her and a meeting took place with Sara Willis, the head of the games staff at Trebizon.

'This is terrible luck, Rebecca,' said Mrs Ericson, tapping the plaster-encased forearm. 'But it's a setback, that's all. It's not the end of the world. Let's sort out a regime that'll keep you fit and help you keep your tennis eye in.'

It was all slightly reassuring. Miss Willis had been in touch with the hospital. There was no reason apparently why Rebecca couldn't do some gentle jogging; she could keep Tish Anderson company. Even better, she'd be permitted to spend all her games periods pounding a tennis ball against the Norris House side wall if she wanted to.

'You've always enjoyed that,' pointed out Miss Willis. 'Keep the bad arm in its sling and treat it as though it doesn't exist. You are *not* to use your left hand. Retrieve the ball, when you have to, with your *right hand*. Next week I'll set up a doubles game for you.'

'Doubles?' asked Rebecca, excited but surprised. 'How? I can't serve – I'm not allowed to throw the ball up.'

'You can bounce the ball off the racket one-handed and do an underarm serve, you'll soon master it. I'll find some volunteers to ball-boy for you so that you're never tempted to pick up the odd ball with that left hand!'

'Why just doubles, why not some singles?' Rebecca said eagerly. 'I mean on the same basis – ball-boys – underarm services.'

'Later, when the plaster's off,' smiled Mrs Ericson. 'You'll be surprised how less mobile you'll feel while that arm's hooked up. Not mobile enough for singles. We use our arms, you know, for balance. We don't want you falling over! You did wonderfully well at Eastbourne, Rebecca,' her coach concluded. 'So cheer up. You'll get over this setback, you know.'

Rebecca lay in bed that night feeling grateful to them both for being so supportive. The prospect of being out of competitive tennis for a whole term was depressing – no matches, no tournaments! Awful, too, to have to watch herself slip down the computer rankings with a long, hard climb back ahead of her after Christmas.

But things weren't quite as black as they'd seemed at first. She was going to be able to keep fit, to keep her eye in – and even play some tennis. Of a sort.

And for this term at least she'd have more time to devote to her GCSE work. Was that what Dad had meant? She might still be able to take the top maths paper. She might still be able to get an A or B grade on her certificate. If she could do that, then some good would have come out of this stupid accident!

She told Robbie so when he cycled over to Court House the next morning.

They went for a walk on the beach together. It had been such a short summer. There was already a wintry look to the grey-green sea, the pale sun lighting up silvery patches towards the skyline, the waves breaking irritably on the shore like ribbons of dirty soap suds.

'Maybe it's all for the best, Robbie. You and Tish never have any problems with maths, do you? Is that what you've applied to do at Oxford?'

'No fear. I don't want to be a mathematician.'

'What then?' asked Rebecca in surprise. 'What have you applied for?'

'PPE,' said Robbie casually. 'It's a really mind-broadening course. Good training for all kinds of careers. Politics, Philosophy and Economics.'

'Are you interested in them then?' asked Rebecca, even more surprised. She could imagine Robbie being interested in economics, but she'd never heard him discuss politics. Or philosophy, come to that!

'Don't know,' Robbie shrugged. 'It's a good course to do.'

'Hey, isn't that what Justy wants to do?' Rebecca vaguely

remembered Sue talking about PPE and Justin Thomas wanting to do it and she'd asked Sue what the letters stood for.

'Right,' said Robbie. 'That's how I got the idea.'

'We've got a Careers Quiz at school this afternoon,' said Rebecca. 'I hope it gives me some ideas.'

Their walk ended and when they reached the foot of the fire escape at the back of Court House, Robbie turned Rebecca round to face him. He looked troubled.

'It's no use your saying it was your fault because of the seat belt. It was my fault. I should have been going slower. I should have remembered about those deer.'

'Oh, Robbie, please don't be silly.'

He shook his head. Then he took out a biro and carefully pulled back the edge of her sling. He wrote on the plaster cast:

SORRY. LOVE, ROBBIE.

It was so touching that Rebecca, to her embarrassment, felt tears of self-pity welling up into her eyes. Robbie turned away abruptly and walked over to his bike. 'Don't cry, Rebeck,' he said edgily. 'Don't you think I feel bad enough already?'

Rebecca tried to speak but he was already scooting his bike along the path, past the dustbins and round the corner of the building out of sight. Not looking back; not wanting her to say any more. He was determined to take the blame. Nothing she said would make any difference.

Now he had gone, Rebecca turned sadly towards the fire escape. With her good hand, she gripped the cold handrail and slowly climbed up the clanking metal treads to the balcony high above.

It was as though there were a barrier between them now.

She let herself in through the heavy glass door at the top, went round into her cubicle and rested on her bed. The plaster round her wrist and forearm made her feel suddenly irritable. It got in the way of things, including her friendship with Robbie. She closed her eyes.

'Miaow!'

The sudden sound made Rebecca jump and for a moment the silly business of the ghost crossed her mind.

'Oh, it's you.'

Moggy sat on the end of her bed, cleaning his ginger and white fur. Then came the sound of whispering and scuffling feet and a red-faced Lizzy Douglas appeared with Kathy Baxter.

'Oops, sorry, Rebecca! Didn't know anyone was up here!' gasped Lizzy, bundling Moggy up in her arms. 'He escaped. We've been looking for him!'

'You're not allowed up here!' said Rebecca crossly. 'I thought it was the ghost cat or something! It made me jump! Clear off.'

As the Third Years retreated, she added:

'And you know pets aren't allowed, Lizzy. He belongs over at Norris with your parents. It's not fair on the others if you have him at Court.'

'Miss Morgan let me have him at Juniper sometimes!'

'Well, you're a *big* girl now, Lizzy,' Rebecca ribbed.

Lizzy's eyes flashed with annoyance for she'd been missing Moggy.

But Rebecca wasn't in a mood to notice.

FOUR

SHADOW IN THE MOONLIGHT

Rebecca hit the tennis ball against the blank side wall of Norris House in a steady rhythm. Backhand, volley, forehand (top spin), drop shot, half-volley and . . . whack! That was a good forehand!

She was feeling cheerful again. There was no sign of the mist that had made the sun so pale on the sea this morning. There'd been clear blue skies this afternoon and a cold little wind had dropped. Now it was a glorious evening. Perhaps they were going to have an Indian summer!

The Careers Quiz for the Fifth Years this afternoon had been fun. The gym had been packed. Some of Trebizon's senior staff had formed a panel to answer questions.

'Is it true you have to be brainy to be a doctor?' Debbie Rickard had asked immodestly. She'd broadcast her ambition to be a doctor some time ago, in the middle of the Fourth Year. At the time Rebecca had wondered if she were merely copying Tish, who'd wanted to be a doctor like her father for as long as

Rebecca could remember. But it seemed genuine enough.

'Yes,' said Mr Douglas briefly. He was in charge of chemistry. 'You also have to be prepared for a long course of study – five years. I dare say you've got what it takes, Deborah.'

She subsided, smirking.

'Remind me not to get ill,' whispered Sue behind her hand.

'I'm ill already,' joked Margot.

'Is it easier to be a vet?' asked Jane McTavish, who loved animals.

'Afraid not, Jane,' said Mr Douglas. 'In fact, at the moment it's harder.'

'Why's that?' chorused several people in surprise.

'It's harder getting *on* to the course,' explained Mr Douglas. 'The competition's tougher. There are more applicants for every place at veterinary school than there are even at medical school. You'd have to think in terms of an A grade in GCSE biology, then another at A level.'

Roberta Jones suddenly looked interested. So did Rebecca. Not because she wanted to be a vet, but because she loved useless facts. Harder to get on a vet course than into medical school!

'Must be because we're such an animal-loving nation,' she whispered to the others.

'And all those vet books,' laughed Tish.

'There's also the question of maths, Jane,' Miss Gates was pointing out gently. 'You'd need a maths A level. And before you could study for that, you'd need to be taking the top paper in GCSE.'

Jane McTavish sank down with a shrug. That clinched it then. She wasn't going to be a vet.

Sue asked Mr Barrington some questions about musical careers; she was a very promising violinist. The questions Rebecca would have liked to ask were questions that had no answer.

How good a tennis player am I going to be? Will I be good enough to turn professional one day? So she said nothing.

Instead, after tea, she collected her racket and ball and ran down the garden to Norris. She'd give the ball a good pounding, just to remind herself she could do it!

Whack! That last ball was a winner; it ricocheted off the wall at a fierce angle. Her speed hampered by the slung-up left arm, Rebecca got only the tip of her racket to it and the thing shot high in the air and landed in the dense shrubbery at the front corner of the building.

Drat. Rebecca ran across and dived into the bushes, poking round with her tennis racket to find the ball. Half doubled up there, she noticed a car pulling up at the front of Norris House, right by Debbie Rickard and Roberta Jones. Idly Rebecca wondered if those two had tentatively started to patch up their quarrel. Although Debbie was now a day girl, she was still formally attached to Norris House. Presumably she'd come back here with Roberta after tea.

'Ready, Deb?' asked her father, from the car. He'd delivered his daughter at school for the Careers Quiz earlier and had now come to pick her up. 'Hello, Berta.'

'Daddy, Berta wondered if she could come back for the evening?' said Debbie cautiously. 'Mrs Douglas says it's OK.'

'Aren't you forgetting something?' frowned Mr Rickard. 'It's English coursework to do this evening.'

He looked as though he had the weight of the world on his shoulders.

'You're right, Dad.'

'Sorry, Berta,' said Debbie's father as he briskly flipped open the car door for his daughter. 'But needs must. I expect you've got a lot of work to do yourself, if you think about it.'

'Oh, yes tons,' said Roberta, red with embarrassment. 'Especially now I've decided on my career.' She took a deep breath. Some compulsion made her say it. 'I've got to work even harder than Debbie. I've decided to be a vet,' she explained airily.

She found it very satisfying, the look on Debbie's face.

When Rebecca told the others later there was mild amusement. Roberta – a vet. It seemed so unlikely.

'She's scared of spiders,' pointed out Elf.

'She was the only one who didn't dare pick up the tortoise when we were First Years – remember?' reminisced Margot.

Rebecca didn't know anything about the tortoise, having been at comprehensive school in London then. But:

'She was just keeping her end up. She'll have forgotten about it by Monday,' she said. At the same time thinking guiltily: Must stop gabbing. Debbie's not the only one with English coursework to do (or her father, come to that). I finished *The Merchant in Venice* last term but I've got the whole of *Jane Eyre* to do this weekend.

Rebecca got down to re-reading *Jane Eyre* the same evening and finally finished her GCSE coursework on it late on Sunday, consulting all the notes she'd taken in lessons the previous term. What a wonderful feeling! To have worked so hard and got it done. To have been so engrossed.

This year they'd be studying some new set books, the ones they'd be tested on in the written exam next summer. The new books looked good, too.

'We won't be doing anything more on *The Merchant of Venice* and *Jane Eyre* now, will we?' Rebecca asked Tish, just before bedtime. She held up last year's exercise book. 'I've finished with all these notes. Are we supposed to keep them? Or shall I just chuck them away?'

'Might as well keep them,' yawned Tish. 'You never know.'

'OK, might as well,' said Rebecca.

Rebecca's first appointment at the hospital was booked for the following Friday. She'd be having a second X-ray to make sure the bones were setting properly. If not, the plaster would have to come off and the whole thing re-set. She dreaded that. And because of the plaster she wasn't sleeping as soundly as usual either.

The night after she'd handed in her English coursework she had a bad dream, heavy with wedding veils and other Victorian resonances of *Jane Eyre*. These were somehow mixed up with the attic quarters at Court House. During the day she loved their new quarters, the sloping ceilings, the rafters, her lovely private cubicle. But at nights, in her present slightly jaded and edgy state, they could seem, well . . . rather spooky.

Rebecca awoke from her dream conscious of a bright square of moonlight on the partition wall; thrown from the glass skylight above. As she stared at it, she felt a prickly sensation in the back of her neck.

Across the square of moonlight on the wall there suddenly glided the black, elongated shadow of a cat. It was only there for a moment. Rebecca ducked under her duvet, then peered out fearfully to see if it would reappear. Had she imagined it? Had it been part of her dream?

'It must have been Moggy,' said Tish, as they went for a short jog on the beach together before breakfast. Tish was already in training for her next race.

'It couldn't have been. It was the wrong shape.'

'But you said it was just its shadow, on the wall,' said Tish sensibly. 'You know how distorted shadows can be.'

'I'd have thought Moggy would be much too fat and lazy to make it to the roof,' mused Rebecca.

'Cats get up to all sorts of things at night,' replied Tish. She laughed. 'Better not tell Mara. She'll be scared stiff! You know what she's like!'

So Rebecca laughed, too. She just knew it wasn't Moggy, so it must have been in the dream! Her imagination had been running away with her! She'd be getting as bad as Mara at this rate.

She was wrong to think Roberta Jones would forget about being a vet.

On the same day as the hospital visit, Roberta came and joined Rebecca's maths division. Miss Hort's brow knitted slightly but she welcomed her and said: 'You can sit in the front, next to Rebecca.' The principal of Trebizon, Miss Welbeck in person, had agreed that she could move up from Division 3 for the time being.

She'd not had much choice. Following a frantic phone call from his daughter, Mr Jones (who knew a lot about golf and vintage port and good cigars but very little about the GCSE) had dictated a long letter to Miss Welbeck insisting that Roberta at least be taught the work required for the top maths paper. It would be wrong of the school to deprive her of any hope of fulfilling her long-cherished ambition to be a vet.

Miss Gates, senior mistress and head of mathematics at Trebizon, had tried to reach him by telephone to point out certain things. But to no avail. He was now away on a business trip and his secretary didn't feel that his ex-wife, who lived elsewhere, would want any say in the matter as she didn't pay the fees. Miss Welbeck felt the school had no choice but to fall in with his wishes for the time being.

'After all, Evelyn, there's no rule that says a person can't take the top paper.'

'None at all, Madeleine,' Miss Gates had responded drily. 'A person can certainly *take* it.'

Rebecca groaned inwardly as Roberta thudded down heavily next to her. *I don't need this*, she thought. Mara shot her a sympathetic glance.

'Now this year of course is GCSE year,' Miss Hort was saying. 'On Monday I'll give out the first of the set tasks that count towards the final grade you get on your certificates next summer. This week we've been revising the work done last year and today we'll go over cylinders again. We shall also deal with pyramids and cones. All of you who want to attempt the top level in the set task will need to know about those.'

Rebecca groaned inwardly again as Roberta said eagerly: 'Please, what's a cylinder?'

And then she groaned out loud when Sujata Seal, who was this year's senior prefect, came to fetch her. Apparently the car was waiting for her at the front of main school. She'd have to brush up on cylinders and pyramids and cones with Mara, later. Or better still, Tish.

It was time to go to the hospital.

FIVE

CLIFF – AND ROBBIE

'Rebecca!' somebody shouted, in total astonishment. '*Rebecca* Mason!'

Rebecca was sitting in out-patients at St Michael's hospital. It was nearly an hour since the X-ray had been taken and she'd been told to wait for the result. Rather than think about it too deeply, she'd looked at several women's magazines and was now reading in paperback *Pride and Prejudice*, one of the new English set books.

She looked up, startled.

A boy of fifteen was swinging in through the main doors on crutches from a car outside, his foot and lower leg encased in plaster, the left leg of his jeans slit open to accommodate it.

Straight brown hair stood up spikily above the cheeky and likeable face. He was laughing at Rebecca in amazement.

'*Cliff!*' squeaked Rebecca. 'Clifford Haynes. I don't believe it. Amanda and Claire *said* you'd moved down here somewhere. But what –' He was sitting down beside her, laying aside his crutches. 'What have you *done?*'

'Hush!' said the sister-in-charge, looking across at them from her desk. 'A little less noise, please.'

Rebecca and Cliff hugged each other. They'd been at primary school in London together, shared a desk when they were little, even gone on to the same comprehensive school. 'Came off the back of a motor bike. Having the plaster off today at long last! And what have *you* done, Rebecca? Look at us two! Talk about the walking wounded.'

They chatted non-stop, trying to remember to keep their voices down. Cliff's Dad had been made redundant in May and he'd got a job selling insurance in the west country, sending Cliff to Caxton High, the good local state school. 'Know it well,' said Rebecca. 'We play your girls in matches. We insult them regularly!'

'And they you,' laughed Cliff. 'It's not bad there except my GCSEs are in a mess.' He pulled a face. 'They're doing a different board here. Take English. We did all these books in London and then before I'd done any coursework, we moved. I get here and all the books are different and then I'm supposed to do all this coursework in the summer holidays. Well, I've been in and out of this place and missed half the lessons last term. I had to have an operation! Now I'm supposed to hand in my coursework soon on last year's books and I've only done about a third!'

'Aren't you getting any help with them?' asked Rebecca sympathetically.

'Everyone's talking about this year's books now. Hey –' he pointed at the paperback on Rebecca's lap. 'Jane Austen, that's one.'

'What were last year's books?' asked Rebecca suddenly.

'Well, Graham Greene, he's not bad. I'm getting on with that all right. And some short stories . . .' He didn't notice that Rebecca was nodding excitedly. 'I like those. But *The Merchant of Venice*! I don't know where to begin with that! And as for *Jane Eyre* –'

'You must be doing the Wessex board like us then!' Rebecca interrupted. 'I thought you must be! Listen, I've still got all my notes – the Shakespeare and the Charlotte Brontë – I'll lend them to you!'

'You wouldn't?' exclaimed Cliff in delight. 'What – all your notes from your lessons? You were brilliant at English, Rebecca. Don't you need them yourself?'

'I've finished with them! I've just handed my coursework in. I was going to chuck my notes away! You can have them!'

'*Would you please keep your voices down,*' they were told. '*There are patients just along the corridor.*'

Then the buzzer went. It was time for Clifford to go through.

'Quick, Cliff, give me your address and I'll post you the notes,' whispered Rebecca, extending her plastered forearm. 'Write it on here!'

He wrote CLIFF in big letters on the plaster, between Robbie's message and Margot's autograph. Then scribbled his address and drew a heart, with the words: R.M. IS WONDERFUL.

Rebecca giggled and waved him goodbye as he hobbled off on his crutches. Less than five minutes later, she was herself summoned to the desk. The sister-in-charge had been handed some notes.

'Doctor's looked at the X-ray now. No problems. No problems at all. Take care not to use that hand, though. Next month we hope to have the plaster off and something a bit more comfortable in its place. I'll ring the school now and they can come and pick you up.'

'Good,' said Mrs Barrington, as they drove back to Trebizon. 'Your grandmother's just been on the phone, asking me how you've got on.' Old Mrs Mason was Rebecca's official guardian in England while her parents were abroad. 'I'll ring her straight back with the news.'

'Will you? Oh, thanks Mrs Barry,' said Rebecca. Next month – what an age. But a load had been lifted from her mind. It was all getting a little easier to bear.

And it had been fun meeting Cliff. Cliff Haynes of all people! She'd parcel those notes up and post them to him, the minute she got back.

When the housemistress dropped her off at Court House she had the whole place to herself. Everyone else was on games. They'd soon be back. It was almost the end of the afternoon. She found a large envelope, rammed the English exercise book inside one-handed and wrote Cliff a note – including the Court House phone number. Maybe he'd ring her up some time and have a chat!

She put a couple of stamps on the envelope and hurried downstairs. If she went over to the pillar-box at main school, she'd just catch the afternoon post. Cliff would get the notes in the morning and could work all weekend if he wanted to!

Girls were starting to stream off the hockey pitches as

47

she walked through the grounds to the pillar-box. On the way back she met up with a track-suited Tish, fresh from First Eleven team practice.

'How did the hospital go, Rebeck?'

'OK,' said Rebecca. 'And I met a boy I used to know! And I've lent him those English notes – well, made him a present. You were right! I *am* glad I kept them. But I missed the whole of maths,' she groaned. 'I wanted to remember about cylinders, let alone cones and pyramids. In fact, I get cones and cylinders muddled up!'

'Rebecca, you're thick!' laughed Tish, pushing her round to the back of Court House. She stopped by the dustbins, lifted a lid and rummaged around.

'What *are* you doing?'

'Pooh. Smells a bit,' said Tish, picking out an empty tin can. 'Let's take it up.'

'Whatever for?' asked Rebecca.

'Well, it's a cylinder, isn't it.'

Upstairs they washed out the dirty tin in the kitchen. Roberta had come back with Jenny and Fiona after hockey. The three of them had been picked for the Second Eleven! Jenny as goalkeeper and the other two as backs and they'd be playing a friendly against Hillstone the next day! They were working out defence tactics and eating some chocolate.

'What you doing with that filthy old can, Tish?' asked Jenny.

'Showing Rebecca about cylinders.'

'Let's see!' exclaimed Roberta.

'Why?' asked Tish in surprise. 'Rebeck missed the lesson, that's all.'

'Come on, Robert,' said Jenny, hauling her back into

the kitchen. 'Get someone at Norris to help you. Let's sort out this match.'

Tish plonked the can on the table where the photocopier was and made Rebecca write down its measurements.

'OK. First – the curved surface area. Well, what's the circumference of a circle?'

'2 pi R,' said Rebecca. 'But what circle?'

'The top of the tin, fathead. That's the circle. Find the circumference of that circle, then multiply it by the height of the tin. Presto – that's it!'

Rebecca borrowed Mara's calculator and worked it out.

'Right! You now know how to find the curved surface area of a cylinder.'

'How easy!' laughed Rebecca, in relief. 'But how do I find its volume?'

'That's just pi R *squared* times height,' said Tish. 'Try it.'

While Rebecca worked it out, Mara produced her notes from the day's lesson. 'Want these copied, Rebecca? It's all here – cones as well. And pyramids. You can learn them and catch up!'

'Thanks, Mara,' said Rebecca as Mara switched on her copy machine with fidgety pleasure. 'I make it 241.9 cubic centimetres, Tish.'

'Sounds about right,' shrugged Tish, bored by now. 'Oi, Mara, run off some for Robert. I get the feeling she didn't understand the lesson.' Roberta was right beside them.

Mara obliged. Tish took the copied notes, shoved them in the old tin can and handed it over with a grin.

'There you are, Robert. The complete kit. All you ever wanted to know about cylinders and never dared ask.'

Roberta took the gift doubtfully. 'What about cones and pyramids?'

'They cost extra,' said Tish, who was off to have a shower. 'Ask the twins,' she added impatiently. 'Or read Mara's notes, can't you?'

Rebecca meanwhile went to her cubicle and put the notes in her maths folder with a little sigh. Cones and pyramids. You had to know about those for the top paper, Miss Hort had reminded them. Was there no end to it?

On Saturday Rebecca and Sue met Robbie and Justin for tea and cakes in Fenners.

Both boys were working like maniacs for their Oxford entrance exams in November. Robbie was taking the maths and physics papers, Justin the history and English papers. Both boys were also taking something called the General Paper, which seemed to prey on their minds.

'That's the one you have to do brilliantly for PPE!' explained Justin. 'You have to prove you've got mental processes of your own and aren't just good at learning things parrot fashion.'

'You have to write four essays in three hours,' mumbled Robbie. 'With lots of ideas in them.'

'Or you can just try and be *profound*,' said Justin. 'Like they had an essay question once that just said: *Why?* And someone simply wrote two words underneath: *Why not?* – and they gave him a place!'

'So rumour has it,' added Robbie sceptically.

Rebecca and Robbie were tending to avoid each other's gaze slightly. She sensed it made him miserable to see her arm still in its sling. She concealed it beneath the table as much as possible, yet still felt edgy herself because he felt edgy.

However, listening to all this talk about Oxbridge with curiosity, she absent-mindedly reached that left hand forward out of its sling to take a slice of chocolate cake. Robbie's eyes darted quickly to the plaster. He saw the heart drawn there and those words . . . CLIFF . . . R.M. IS WONDERFUL.

When they had to get back because Sue had orchestra, Robbie suddenly whispered to Rebecca, in a strained voice: 'Who's Cliff?'

'Oh. Nobody in particular,' said Rebecca, taken by surprise.

As the two friends approached Court House by the back way, they saw Lizzy Douglas had her ground-floor window open: and Moggy was sitting on the window-sill. As she stroked him, Mrs Barrington called out from the garden:

'Now what's he doing round here again? Take him back to your parents. I've told you not to encourage him, Lizzy.'

'I don't encourage him, Mrs Barry! I don't do anything! I can't help it if he just comes round, can I?'

As Rebecca and Sue went upstairs, Sue said with a laugh: 'Didn't she look guilty? Lizzy!' But Rebecca was thinking about other matters.

Things seemed to be getting more awkward between her and Robbie, not less.

SIX

ACTION COMMITTEE!

Rebecca slogged on with her school work. Robbie rang up from time to time a little stiffly, inquiring about the arm.

By October she was starting to count the days, looking forward to being rid of the cumbersome plaster and the sling. Soon after that would come half-term, five whole days' holiday. She'd spend it at her grandmother's bungalow in Gloucestershire. She was looking forward to that, too.

This is silly, she told herself, wishing time away like this. Why do I feel so jaded?

As someone who was naturally athletic and bursting with physical energy, she was missing hockey and tennis and being in the fresh air and falling into bed pleasantly exhausted each night. The tennis doubles fixed up by Miss Willis once a week she found merely frustrating. She couldn't really move around the court freely: it was such a nuisance being hampered like this. It was stupid having to serve underarm! She preferred pounding the tennis ball against the wall of Norris but that had its limits.

No tennis. No hockey. No netball. No swimming. Elf patiently played table tennis with her a few times but even that was awkward. Tish was now jogging along the beach too fast and too far for Rebecca. She was racing in London at half-term – at a big indoor meeting!

Rebecca felt frowzy, as though she were winding down, running to seed. Enervated. Cooped up with her books, her school work – and especially her GCSE coursework – simply stretched itself out soggily to fill the time available and take twice as long as it needed to.

But she would get that good GCSE maths grade or die!

The printed booklets for the first set task had been issued to all Fifth Year pupils. Div 3 girls mainly did only the first paper, which could earn them an E, F or G grade, although those who wanted to try for a C or D grade did the second paper, too. In Div 2, Rebecca's, everyone did both papers and some the top paper as well, if they were aiming for an A or B. In Div 1 they did all three papers and a few did an 'extension' paper which could earn them a distinction. It was tucked away at the end of the booklet and contained, to Rebecca, incomprehensible problems involving ship navigation and non-factorizable quadratic equations.

'There's some calculus and logic, too,' Tish had grinned. 'It's good fun.'

Rebecca was relieved to find that she could complete the top paper and so was not yet knocked out of the running for an A or B grade. Roberta Jones, too, had been equally determined. She mustn't stumble at the first hurdle! Not if she wanted to be a vet!

It was all very well for the crowd at Court, she thought. They were so easy going. Fiona had told her how Tish Anderson had knocked off the whole booklet, sitting at the big table one Sunday afternoon with half the floor gathered round her. Then left it lying there for days for her friends to consult if they wanted to! Getting help at Norris was quite a different story.

Joss Vining was brilliant at maths but was never there! Now she was in the England 18 hockey group she was always dashing off somewhere or other. Also she glided along on her own rarified plane of calculus (was it?) and when Roberta had asked her about cones she'd told her to go and buy an ice-cream at Moffat's.

As for the Nathan twins, they were useless. They'd lectured her:

'It's no use our helping you, Berta. You'll only fail the authenticity test. Then Miss Hort will mark your course-work right down anyway.'

'But you help each other!'

'That's different.'

'We're twins!'

And as for Debbie. She wasn't just useless, she was worse than useless. It just wasn't a bit fair, all the help she was getting when she didn't even need it! Well, she'd show her . . . she'd show Debbie!

And the morning they handed their coursework in and were given the authenticity test in class, Rebecca noticed that Roberta, too, had a well filled-up top paper – she seemed to have completed most of it.

The test was a short written one, designed by the examination board. It was called an authenticity test because it would show whether a pupil had actually understood the coursework they'd just handed in, or whether they'd been given a lot of help.

As Rebecca scribbled down the answers, she suddenly became conscious that Roberta was copying her. *How pathetic*, she thought and wondered who Roberta had found to do her coursework for her.

Rebecca was pleased to be eventually awarded a B grade for that first set task. Even the fact that Roberta got a B, too, couldn't mar her pleasure.

Miss Hort was already distributing a second printed booklet to the class, a much thicker one. This was known as 'the extended set task' and contained about eight hours' work. It was the most important piece of coursework and if completed could earn up to 25 per cent of the entire GCSE maths mark.

The Fifth Years would all have four weeks to do it in: they could take it home over half-term if they wanted to. This coursework would require more than a simple authenticity test after it had been handed in. Each girl would be given a five-minute oral examination by the teacher, privately, on a one-to-one basis, to see if she'd really understood the work.

'Robert won't be able to cheat next time, will she, Rebecca?' Mara pointed out, not without satisfaction. 'The oral will be *horrible*!'

'Don't remind me,' laughed Rebecca. 'You and I had better get our act together, never mind Robert.'

'Bobbie, it's Daddy here. I'm back home now. I thought I'd better give you a ring. I found this letter waiting for me from your Miss Gates, about your maths GCSE. Something about if you take the top paper and do badly you could get a FAIL, but if you just take the lower papers you can earn yourself a C grade next summer and that's not bad –'

'A C grade's no use!' said Roberta petulantly. 'I've got to get an A or a B if I want to be a vet. I've told you that, Daddy! Besides, I'm already on the way. We had the marks for our first piece of coursework this week. I got a B!'

'By jove, you amaze me. Well done, poppet.'

'Rebecca? It's Cliff here. I said I'd ring. Did you get my letter?'

He'd written to her last month to thank her for the English notes and to say how useful they looked.

'Were they any help?' Rebecca asked cautiously. 'How did it go?'

'Rebecca, you're not going to believe this, but I got a *B*!'

'Cliff!' shrieked Rebecca in delight. 'You didn't!'

'Those notes were ace,' he said gratefully. 'Talk about shedding light in dark corners. I even read the books after that. *Jane Eyre*'s good once you get into it; a bit creepy in places. And after getting to grips with *The Merchant of Venice*, I'm finding *Romeo and Juliet* quite easy!'

Romeo and Juliet was one of the new set books for next summer's exam.

'It's all down to Miss Heath,' said Rebecca. 'She's a fantastic English teacher, she really is. I got an A for those books! I'm so glad I've got her for these two years.'

'An A? Brilliant. I think we should go some place and have a little celebration. I'll buy you some beer!'

'I don't drink, Cliff,' laughed Rebecca.

'Well, can't we go out one evening?'

'How?'

'Oh, you're in Holloway prison, I keep forgetting. When's your next trip to hospital?'

'Three weeks on Friday, three o'clock in the afternoon,' Rebecca replied promptly. The time and date were imprinted on her mind in letters of fire. 'Why?'

'That's when I go to physio! Every Friday afternoon!' exclaimed Cliff. 'I'll look out for you!'

'I'm having the plaster off that day,' explained Rebecca.

'Brilliant again,' said Cliff. 'Double celebration. I'll hang around till you come out. See you then. I'll think of something good!'

Rebecca ground on with her school work. Maths . . . biology. She'd dropped physics and chemistry, thanks to failing the summer exams so badly. That gave her more time for history and geography, which both had a huge amount of coursework. And her best subjects: Latin, French and German. There was no written coursework for those, just some oral work in the spring term. Then big exams next summer!

Debbie Rickard was doing brilliantly at everything. Her geography coursework was dazzling.

But Mrs Beal frowned and deducted quite a lot of marks in the confidential record sheet that would eventually be sent up to the examination board.

'It was quite obvious that her father had helped her a great deal,' she told her friend Miss Heath in the staff room.

'I'm afraid he's been interfering with her English, too,'

sighed Miss Heath. 'I was fully expecting her to get an A but I had to mark it down to a B. Such a shame. But it was full of adult comments that didn't really relate to the questions set. Do you know – he phoned me next day and complained about his grade!'

They both laughed.

'Let's hope he doesn't insist on coming to school and writing her exam papers for her next summer,' Mrs Beal said drily. 'That would really ruin her chances.'

'But I wish the Rickards hadn't done this,' said Miss Heath, serious now. 'Moving house to be practically on top of the school. Luckily the rest of the Fifths don't have their parents breathing down their necks.'

Rebecca and the rest of 'the six' at least were certainly well satisfied with their life as boarders on the attic floor of Court House.

They could retreat to the peace and quiet of their partitioned cubicles when they needed to work, with just the sound of the birds twittering in the eaves above their windows; at other times make tea, play with the copy machine, talk about their coursework – and celebrate the A grades as they came along. Tish and Sue seemed to get one after another! Sue had to compose four little pieces of music and had got all As so far. Margot and Elf were shining in science. Rebecca had got all As and Bs to date – and Mara wasn't doing badly, either. Like Rebecca, she'd managed a B for that first maths task! The second one, the 'extended set task', was looking a bit more daunting.

But the lack of exercise was getting Rebecca down. She wasn't properly tired when she went to bed at night.

And she still wasn't sleeping soundly.

Sometimes she would wake up in the middle of the night and hear funny little creaks and rattles. It was quite eerie. There was somebody walking about on the roof above her head – she'd swear there was! Perhaps it was the ghost of that Victorian schoolmaster – or else his cat!

Then one night, lying on her back and staring up at the black square of skylight above, she saw two pinpricks of light, luminous in the darkness. There was a pair of eyes up there, staring down at her unblinkingly, boring into her!

The moon suddenly slid out from between two clouds and Rebecca saw it at last – the cat.

It certainly wasn't Mr and Mrs Douglas's Moggy.

It was skeletally thin, ghostly grey in colour and all eyes – wild-looking, luminous green eyes, glaring down at her through the glass of the skylight. It was truly startling. Rebecca shuddered. If the cat could appear, she thought, beset by night imaginings in those scary small hours, might its master not be far behind?

She turned over and hid her face in the pillow, heart beating fast, and told herself fiercely that she didn't believe in ghosts and it was time to get back to sleep.

This time she told all the others about it, she couldn't stop herself. She told them at breakfast. On the next table, a crowd from Norris listened in fascination.

'It must be a stray,' said Elf.

'Action Committee!' said Margot. They always called themselves that when there was a mystery to solve.

'I shall tell Sarah Turner what I think of her!' said Mara, with a slight shiver. 'I shall tell her off for making up such a horrible story last Christmas!'

In fact, the Lower Sixth girl simply laughed in Mara's face.

However, in spite of the fact that the six searched high and low for the next two days, and asked lots of people about it including the domestic staff, there was neither sight nor sound of a stray cat at Trebizon nor ever had been.

SEVEN

TWO DISCOS

At last the day came for Rebecca to have the plaster off. And she'd be seeing Cliff again! Mrs Barrington dropped her off at St Michael's hospital on the Friday afternoon, then rushed off to do some shopping. She'd come back later.

'Well, Rebecca, how does that feel?' smiled the doctor as the hated plaster cast was cut away.

'Lovely!' exclaimed Rebecca, extending her left arm. She gazed at it in wonder and gingerly clenched and unclenched her left fist. It felt rather wobbly and numb from the elbow down to the palm of the hand but that was only to be expected. 'It feels lovely!'

The doctor made a careful examination, gave a satisfied nod and then handed Rebecca over to a nursing sister, who rolled a thick, firm elastic bandage over the heel of Rebecca's hand and half-way up the arm. 'This'll give you support now,' she said. 'It's been a nasty one. A multiple fracture. You're going to need quite a lot of physiotherapy. But you'll be playing games again by Christmas.'

It had been fixed for Rebecca to have these sessions up

at school, under Trebizon's own insurance scheme. She'd need them every day at first!

She wandered out into the reception area, keeping her eyes open for Cliff.

'Do you want to sit down and wait for your lift?' asked the sister-in-charge.

'No, it's all right!' Rebecca said suddenly. She'd just seen Cliff! 'I'll wait outside, thanks.'

The main doors were open and she could see Cliff jumping up and down like a jumping bean, waving and grinning, in the street outside.

'Rebecca!'

'Cliff!'

He grabbed her by the hand, laughing:

'Look at us, don't we look fine!'

'You've got your leg back!'

'And you've got your arm back!'

Cliff tugged her along the pavement to the shelter of the striped blind over Brills, the baker's shop. 'Come under here, it's pouring!'

'I hadn't even noticed!' laughed Rebecca. She felt lightheaded and carefree. She'd got rid of that terrible encumbrance at last! She didn't need the sling any more, either! She pressed her nose against the shop window. 'Oh, Cliff. Look at those cakes. I want one of those delicious custard tarts!'

'I'll get one for you, Rebecca! And one for myself at the same time!'

They sheltered under the awning, munched their custard tarts and giggled. Rebecca was keeping her eyes open for Mrs Barry's car. They weren't supposed to eat in the street!

'Well, I've got it all worked out,' said Cliff. He produced a ticket from his pocket and handed it to Rebecca. 'Here you are. I've paid for it. It's the least I owe you. And we'll really rave, babe!'

'What is it?' asked Rebecca, reading the ticket. 'Disco –?'

'School disco!' commanded Cliff. 'Tomorrow fortnight. Saturday night rave-up at Caxton High.'

He jumped up and down and spun round and round on the rainy pavement, laughing. 'Look – I can dance – I've got my leg back!'

Rebecca giggled, feeling excited.

'It's just after half-term! We get back on the Thursday evening. I wonder if Mrs Barry'd let me go?'

'She's got to! Lots of people come. I've paid three quid for the ticket now, so she'll have to let you!'

'Here she is now!' exclaimed Rebecca. They quickly brushed the crumbs off their clothes and looked straight-faced.

As the housemistress parked the car by the hospital, Rebecca and Cliff walked back there along the pavement. Mrs Barry got out.

'Hello, Rebecca. Everything go all right?'

She glanced at Cliff.

'It went fine. Mrs Barry, this is Cliff – Clifford Haynes. We've known each other since we were six! He lives down here now and he's at Caxton High and –' the last words came out in a rush '– please can I go to their school disco tomorrow fortnight?'

The housemistress frisked the boy with her eyes. He looked pleasant, she thought. He gave her a winning smile – half cheeky, half cherubic.

'All right,' she said promptly. 'I can run you to the High School.' She always liked to make quite sure that her girls arrived safely at their claimed destinations. 'But what about getting back?'

'My mother'll run Rebecca back!' Cliff said promptly.

'Right,' said Mrs Barry. She opened the car door for Rebecca. 'And she'd have to be back by eleven o'clock and no later.'

Before driving off, she wound down the window and said lightly: 'Would your mother mind dropping me a note, just to confirm that arrangement? Mrs Joan Barrington, Court House, Trebizon School. I'm sorry to put her to the trouble, but it *is* a rule.'

'She'll be pleased to, Mrs Barrington,' Cliff responded quickly.

He waved Rebecca out of sight and she waved back. Then, fingering the ticket that was safely in her pocket, she said:

'Thanks, Mrs Barry! Thanks!'

Secretly the housemistress was pleased to see the colour back in Rebecca's cheeks. She'd been pale and listless, cooped up indoors so much, missing her sports. He looked a nice lad and the school disco would be a properly run affair. An evening out would do Rebecca good. But aloud she said:

'Mind you get that big piece of maths coursework done in good time. Doesn't it have to be in on the Monday morning?'

'I'm half-way through it already, Mrs Barry,' responded Rebecca self-righteously. 'And if I haven't finished it by half-term, I'll take it back to Gran's with me and finish it there.'

*

Rebecca confided in Mara the same afternoon and showed her the ticket.

'I'll buy something new to wear while I'm at Gran's!' said Rebecca. 'Something disco-ish!'

'Me, too,' said Mara, her brown eyes aglow. 'I shall get Aunty Papademas to buy me something in London. I'm going to a disco that night as well. Curly has asked me!'

'Are they having a disco at Garth then?' Rebecca asked quickly. 'Just a Fifth Year disco, I suppose,' she probed.

Curly Watson, the light of Mara's life, was a month younger than Mara and in the Fifth. Unlike Robbie Anderson, now a lordly Upper Sixth.

'No, all the seniors . . .' began Mara, then broke off, quickly reading the furrow that had crossed Rebecca's brow.

'Well, Robbie hasn't asked me to *that*!' she was thinking. 'Now I'm twice as glad I agreed to go to Cliff's.'

'Don't look cross with Robbie!' Mara was saying. 'He thinks of nothing but Oxbridge at the moment! All those boys who are doing it are the same! I've heard them talking in Fenners! Curly has promised me he is *not* going to do it. Where is this Oxbridge? He's not even going to do A levels. He is going to join the navy!'

Rebecca giggled then.

'I could just see Curly in bell-bottomed trousers. They'd suit him!'

At that moment Tish burst on to the scene, wearing her track-suit and looking flustered and bad-tempered. She'd just had First Eleven team practice again.

'I can't find my spikes!' she said. 'I'm in a hurry. I've got to go down to the track before tea and Miss Willis kept us for ages –'

She was sorting through a pile of sports stuff that tended to get flung in the corner by the big table. Not only was she training frenetically for her big race in London at half-term but Trebizon's First Eleven was taking part in a two-day hockey tournament that same week. Thank goodness they didn't clash, she'd said.

'– *and* to crown it all,' Tish was saying, 'that clot-headed Robert the Robot accosted me and begged me to pop over to Norris and help her with her coursework. Just a few little things she didn't understand! Would only take a few minutes! A few weeks, more like it . . . Ah! Found them!'

Tish's bad temper evaporated as quickly as it had come, as she hauled a pair of running shoes out from the bottom of the pile. She leaned against the big table and started to put them on.

'You look great, Rebecca! They took the plaster off then? How did it go?'

'Fine,' said Rebecca. 'When are you going to do *your* coursework, Tish?' she inquired.

'After half-term, of course,' said Tish, tightening up her laces. 'The weekend we're back.'

'Not going to the Garth disco, then?' Rebecca asked casually. She'd decided she wasn't going to mention her own invitation to Caxton High. Not just yet, anyway.

'Oh, I'm going to *that*,' said Tish. 'Edward's asked me. But that's nothing! That doesn't take the whole weekend! Bye, Rebeck. Bye, Mara. See you at tea.'

Edward, thought Rebecca. Sue's brother – in the Upper Sixth like Robbie. Well, he was working hard, too, but that wasn't stopping *him* going to the disco. And what was the betting that Justy had asked Sue? Oh, well, she didn't care. It would be great to go to Cliff's. But she wouldn't say anything to the others about it, just at the moment. She'd tell Mara not to say anything.

As for Tish's coursework! That was cutting things a bit fine, wasn't it? Even for Tish.

'You going to ring Robbie and let him know how it went at the hospital?' asked Sue.

It was the same evening. Rebecca had been sitting on her bed, propped against the pillows, checking her translation, Chapter 7, Nero and Agrippina, hoping that Mr Pargiter was going to like it. Sue had been practising her violin in her cubie opposite and Tish kept popping in and out of the bathroom, washing her hair or something. They seemed to have the floor to themselves.

'Does it look like it?' asked Rebecca.

Her arm was aching rather badly and she was glad that the physiotherapy exercises, which would help get everything right again, were to start the next day. She'd felt envious as she'd watched Margot and Elf and a whole crowd of them go over to the sports centre to play badminton; listened to Tish as she went off to have a bath, stretching luxuriously and saying: 'I feel totally exhausted and deliciously fit and I'm going to have a bath.'

She'd been sitting there wondering whether to have an early night, feeling listless and yet not properly tired.

'Robbie can ring me if he wants to know how it went at the hospital!' Rebecca added.

'He thinks you're fed up with him,' said Sue. She'd taken her glasses off and was polishing them. 'According to Justy that is. He thinks you're fed up with him and so he's keeping a low profile.'

'That's stupid! And it's still up to him to ring *me* and not the other way round,' repeated Rebecca stubbornly. 'After all!' she blurted out crossly. 'It was *his* emergency stop.'

Tish, hoving into view in her dressing-gown, rubbing her damp dark curls with a towel, stopped dead. She and Sue exchanged looks, raised their eyebrows, but said nothing. Did Rebecca after all secretly resent what had happened? Did she, in spite of all her protestations, secretly blame Robbie? It was all quite understandable. What a terrible bore that stupid accident had been!

Rebecca closed her eyes. She was surprised at her own outburst. She would like to have bitten her tongue off. But she was wondering the same thing herself.

EIGHT

A MAGISTERIAL FIGURE

Rebecca enjoyed half-term at her grandmother's. Thank goodness she'd had the plaster off in time. Gran would have fussed horribly to see her arm in a sling like that. As it was she clucked about the elastic bandage being so dirty and wanted to wash it. Finally she took Rebecca to her own doctor and had a new, clean, firm one fitted.

Although the physiotherapy sessions at school had been making the wrist and fingers ache, they seemed to be working; it was all feeling much better now.

'When's that film going to be on?' asked Gran.

The film about Trebizon, with Rebecca playing a 'starring role', had been ready for some weeks but apparently it still awaited the appropriate television slot.

'Looks like the Christmas holidays now,' said Rebecca.

'Good! You'll be home and we can watch it together. You can make sure I work the machine properly,' she added, glancing fearfully at the video recorder. 'I wiped my cookery programme off by accident last week, drat it.'

Rebecca finished off her maths coursework at half-term, the 'extended set task'. She managed to complete the whole of the top paper with the exception of two questions on vectors. She also caught up with biology, learnt some German vocabulary – and bought a new outfit for the disco!

After all, Cliff had said it was a good way of celebrating and you couldn't have a proper celebration in some dingy old outfit! The skirt was darkish and the new length; the matching shirt had lovely floppy cuffs which would go a long way to hiding her stupid bandage.

She returned to school in good spirits after tea on the Thursday and found everyone else very cheerful, too. Tish had come fifth in the London race. She'd had her photo in one of the newspapers as the youngest competitor, who apparently 'showed great promise'! The hockey tournament had been exciting too: the Trebizon First Eleven had been runners-up!

'Joss was in the most amazing form,' said Sue, who'd gone along to watch both days.

Mara had managed to get that new outfit out of Mrs Papademas! She was parading up and down the long aisle between the cubicles, showing it off to everyone like a mannequin.

'Only two days till the disco!' she said happily.

'I'll feel like Cinderella in my old denim skirt,' grumbled Tish, who'd been too busy lately to think about clothes. 'But your brother wouldn't notice if I were wearing a sack, would he, Susan?'

'Uh?' said Sue, who was gazing anxiously in her cubie mirror and wondering what to do about a spot on her cheek.

'I've bought something myself over half-term,' began Rebecca, plonking her holdall on the bed, ready to unzip it. She was longing to show the others her new outfit, and had decided that keeping mum about going to the disco with Cliff had gone on quite long enough. She'd tell them! What was wrong with it?

But at that moment Elf burst in through the double doors at the end, puffing. She'd run all the way up the stairs from the ground floor, where she'd been watching TV with Margot and Jenny.

'Rebecca. Phone for you. It's Robbie.'

Rebecca noticed that Tish and Sue exchanged interested glances.

She went hesitantly downstairs to the phone.

'Hello, Robbie. How's the Oxbridge work going?' she asked him. 'It's only three weeks now, isn't it?'

She'd already questioned Tish about it and been told that Robbie had shut himself in his room for most of half-term with his maths and physics books.

'Terrible. I feel like a zombie. Rebecca, Tish says you've got the plaster off and you're having physio. I did think about the disco on Saturday but then I thought with your arm . . .'

As his voice trailed off lamely, Rebecca gave a little snort. Tish and Sue had put him up to this! He hadn't thought about her arm, he hadn't thought about the disco, he hadn't thought about anything except his stupid Oxbridge . . .

'I don't dance on my hands, Robbie.'

'Oh, Rebeck, I'm sorry,' he said, in a sudden little rush. 'I can't act to save my life. I never even thought about the disco, I'm in such a blur at the moment –'

'Or my arm!' said Rebecca.

'That's not true,' he retorted fiercely. 'I wish it had happened to *me*, if you really want to know. If only I'd been going a bit slower –'

'Oh, Robbie, don't go through that again,' said Rebecca gently. She was feeling mean now. 'Everything's fine. It really is. The exercises are good – it's almost better.'

'Is it? Is it really? Do you feel like coming to the disco then?'

Rebecca's mouth had gone dry. She licked her lips.

'Robbie, it's so stupid. I haven't been anywhere all term and now two things are happening on the same night . . .'

'What d'you mean?'

'Well, there's this boy I know from London, we've known each other since we were little. He's sweet, he's really good fun –' She was gabbling it out as fast as possible. 'Well, he's moved down here – isn't that amazing? – and I said I'd go to this disco at his school . . .'

There was a heavy silence. Then Robbie said:

'Oh, OK. Fine. That's fine. I'll give ours a miss, then. I've got a stack of revision to do anyway.'

'Robbie. He's –' Rebecca was trying to get the words out; trying to say: *Robbie, he's only a friend.*

But Robbie had already hung up.

The disco at Caxton High School was wonderful fun! 'You look great, Rebecca!' Tish had shouted to her before she left.

While the rest of them had rushed around the top floor getting ready, Tish had sat calmly at the big table polishing off the last of her maths coursework. She'd only started it on the Friday and already it was finished! 'Now I can enjoy myself at Garth!' she'd laughed exuberantly, diving off to her cubicle to get changed. 'I'll leave it out in case any of you want to look at it tomorrow!'

'What good is that?' Mara had sighed. 'Miss Hort would soon catch us out when she gives us the oral next week!'

Tish had kept the minibus waiting. Running to catch it, she'd shouted out that compliment to Rebecca, who was just climbing into Mrs Barry's car at the front of Court House.

Rebecca knew she looked all right and it added zest to the evening. Cliff was certainly an energetic dancer! It was quite a challenge keeping up with him! But Rebecca was no slouch herself because towards the end of the night a crowd gathered round and watched them and clapped. The music was good. The youths from Dennizon Point who ran the disco had the best collection of records Rebecca had heard for ages!

Cliff, who had a lucrative paper round as well as a Saturday job, kept treating Rebecca to things. Endless glasses of Coke to quench her thirst, several strips of raffle tickets and six turns on the tombola!

She won two boxes of chocolates, a bottle of sherry and a huge stuffed dog!

'What am I going to do with all these?' giggled Rebecca as she stacked them on a chair. 'Cliff, let me buy you something! Let me buy you some crisps.' That was about all she could afford after spending so much on her outfit.

'You know something, Rebecca,' said Cliff as they munched the crisps and actually sat out a whole session:

'It was the best stroke of luck I ever had, meeting you at the hospital this term. It's really changed my luck, those notes of yours. Mrs Entwistle had just been ignoring me, I think she thought I was thick, but now I've moved up to Mr Patrick's group for English and it's really good. So that's two GCSEs I'm going to get for a start. English and English lit.'

'Well, you never had any trouble with maths,' remembered Rebecca. 'So that's three!'

The DJ announced the last session.

'Come on, Rebecca!'

Some fast and furious rock and roll, a moony dance to end with and then balloons were floating down from the ceiling and everyone was hurling streamers over everyone else! It was all finished.

It was nearly eleven o'clock.

'We'd better get you back,' said Cliff, putting his anorak round her shoulders. 'Tom will be waiting for us outside.'

Tom was Cliff's twenty-two-year-old brother, a trainee accountant. Mrs Haynes had written to Rebecca's housemistress explaining that she and her husband were going to the theatre in Exonford on the night of the disco, but that her elder son Tom, a sensible driver who had his own car, would get Rebecca back to school by eleven.

But when they got outside, mingling with the quickly dispersing crowd, there was no sign of Tom. All the other cars and minibuses soon roared away, leaving them standing there alone.

It was raining gently and they stood there getting damper and damper, clutching Rebecca's prizes, scanning the school drive anxiously for some sign of the headlights, some sign of a late arrival.

'Is he always late?' asked Rebecca, feeling anxious. It was well past eleven now! Everybody had gone! The three youths from Dennizon Point were packing all their disco equipment into an old van. Any moment now the caretaker would be locking up and the whole place would be plunged into darkness.

'No, never,' said Cliff. 'Reliable to a fault, is Tom. Always showing me up. Oh flip, what's happened to him? The car must have conked out on the way here.'

They heard the sound of the van's engine starting up. The disco was leaving! 'Quick!' said Cliff, giving Rebecca a little push.

They rushed over to the moving van, Cliff banging on the side.

'Can you give us a lift?' he begged.

'Oh, give over. Take a look in the back. You can see how loaded up her is.'

'We'll give you a bottle of sherry!' exclaimed Rebecca, holding it up and at the same time producing her best smile. 'And we're not very big. Are we, Cliff?'

The sound of brakes.

'You're on!'

It was an excruciatingly uncomfortable ride, bumping along in that little van, doubled up amongst loudspeakers, electrical wiring, coloured spotlights, a strapping west countryman – and Cliff. But Rebecca didn't care! As long as she could get back to school!

The van took them a good way up Trebizon's school drive and then at Rebecca's request dumped them off by some bushes, near the footpath that cut through the shrubbery to Court House. Them and the two boxes of chocolates and the huge stuffed dog.

'How you getting back, Cliff?' whispered Rebecca as the van reversed and lurched off.

'Don't worry! It's less than two miles – I can walk. Look – it's stopped raining and there's some moonlight now. Let's get you in safely. Will you get into trouble?'

It was a quarter to midnight.

'We've got a fire escape!' whispered Rebecca. 'I can get in that way!'

They crept round to the back of Court House. 'I'll help you up to the top with all this stuff!' whispered Cliff. He was holding the dog which they'd christened Bonzo. 'You'll never manage!'

'Sssh!' smiled Rebecca, as they tiptoed up the iron treads of the exterior staircase, trying hard to stop them from clanking. 'Everyone's in bed.'

The whole of Court House was in darkness, top floor included. The others must have got back from Garth some time ago! They reached the metal balcony and Cliff shook the dog in Rebecca's face, grinning. 'Woof!' he hissed. Somehow Rebecca managed not to giggle out loud.

'You've still got a streamer in your hair!' he mouthed. He pulled it out and put it round her neck. 'There! Suits you.'

'Isn't it lovely up here?' she whispered.

They stood on the balcony and gazed at the sky. Now the rain clouds had moved away there were quite a few stars out up there.

She kissed Cliff on the cheek.

'Thanks for a great evening,' she whispered. 'Ring me tomorrow and let me know if Tom's all right.'

He put an arm round her shoulders, gave her a hug, then removed his anorak and tiptoed away backwards down the metal steps.

Rebecca leaned over the balcony and whispered down:

'Romeo, Romeo, wherefore art thou Romeo?'

Cliff shook with laughter at the foot of the steps, looked up and gave her a wave.

'On the way home, Juliet!'

She waved back as he tiptoed past the ground-floor windows, rounded the corner of the building and disappeared from sight.

She lingered on the balcony for another minute or two, just gazing. She held in her arms the stuffed toy and the boxes of chocolates, her hair still damp from the rain. Breathing in the scents of the night, she pulled the narrow ribbon of streamer from her neck, held it between thumb and finger, then pretended she was dancing again, twirling around a few times, fluttering the streamer. At last, with a smile, she dropped it over the edge of the balcony and watched it drift slowly down towards the moonlit garden below.

Goodbye, disco! Goodbye, lovely evening!

She felt a glow she hadn't felt for weeks, a pleasant feeling of physical exhaustion.

The streamer fell to earth and she lifted her head. It was time to go to bed. One last look across the gardens, across to the dark bulk of Norris House . . .

She gasped out loud.

A little tremor of fear ran through her.

By the line of dark sycamore trees that lay on the far side of Norris House, she glimpsed a figure of Victorian stiffness silhouetted there. A tall and truly magisterial figure wearing something that billowed from the shoulders – a schoolmaster's gown? Even from this distance he seemed to be stern, unbending. Gazing towards Court House with an air of Victorian disapproval.

Rebecca closed her eyes in disbelief and when she opened them the figure had gone. 'Was I dreaming or what?' she wondered, her heart banging away in her chest. She was too scared to wait and see if the figure would reappear.

She turned away, slipped in through the glass door and closed it softly behind her. The whole floor was in darkness but she could hear the comforting sounds of breathing along the line of cubicles. It was nice to be back indoors!

She felt her way carefully along the big table, her own footsteps scaring her as the floorboards creaked. Then round the corner into her cubicle.

'Is that you, Rebeck?' whispered Tish sleepily from behind her partition wall in the corner there. 'You all right? We pretended to Mrs Barry you were back!'

'I'm all right!' whispered Rebecca, her throat feeling dry. 'Night, Tish!'

'Night, Rebecca!'

Shivering slightly, Rebecca dumped her stuff on the floor, donned her pyjamas in the dark and quickly scrambled into bed.

NINE

THE FUR FLIES

Sheer physical exhaustion overwhelmed Rebecca but her sleep was troubled. Within the hour she was wide awake again. Something had woken her up.

It was an eerie little sound – a mewing sound.

She stared at the skylight above.

A pair of green eyes stared back.

Then she heard another sound, just the other side of her cubie wall, the door to the fire escape side. A curious swishing sound like the swish of a gown. Then came the sound of creaking floorboards. There was somebody moving about on the other side of the partition!

She lay rigid, fear crawling all over her. For thirty seconds she lay there, too terrified to move. She wanted to cry out but she couldn't. As she held her breath, gazing up at the skylight, the luminous eyes vanished and there came little creaks and whispering sounds as the cat descended the roof.

Was it coming in here? Coming to join its master?

'Don't be such a fool, fool, *fool*,' she told herself,

clenching at her duvet cover. 'It was only a *joke*. There aren't any ghosts, there *aren't*.'

She tried not to think about that figure she'd seen by the distant sycamore trees. She swallowed hard.

'Who's that moving around?' she called out at last, in a dry little voice. 'That you, Tish?'

Hurried footsteps. Loudly creaking boards. A scuffling noise.

'Whoever you are, you're not supposed to be here!' Rebecca cried out bravely. 'I'm going to put the light on!'

There came a sudden little rush of cold air; the outer door must have been opened. And then –

An unearthly cry of pain! Followed by –

YEEEOOOWWWWW!

A terrible caterwauling.

Like a flying blur of grey fur, the skeletal cat rose high in the air and came over the top of the partition wall. Coming straight at her with claws outstretched, eyes blazing and teeth bared.

Rebecca dived under cover as it landed, spitting, on her back.

And screamed for help.

Lights went on. Her friends scrambled out of bed. The cat had already disappeared.

Sue put Rebecca's light on and found her sitting propped against the pillows, duvet clutched round her chin, white-faced and frightened.

'Had a nightmare, Becky?' asked Sue anxiously, the first to reach her side.

'No, it was real!' gasped Rebecca. 'It was the grey cat! And earlier I saw this figure, wearing a kind of gown!

Over by the trees. And it was in the room just now, I heard it. And the cat! It came straight at me.' She pointed, still trembling slightly, to the top of her partition wall. 'It came at me from up there. Somebody threw it over my cubie wall, threw it at me!'

'What, the same cat you saw before?' asked Margot.

'You've just had a bad dream,' said Elf gently. 'I'll get you a hot drink –'

'Dream my foot!' exclaimed Tish, rounding the corner into Rebecca's quarters. 'The fire escape door's wide open. Someone's been here all right!'

They made a great fuss of Rebecca while she drank some hot milk, keeping their voices low so as not to wake the rest of the floor.

Mara was petrified and refused to get out of bed at all.

'Well, I've managed to get both the bolts across at last,' said Tish, after a while. 'We really must ask Mrs Barry to get them seen to.' The bolts were very stiff, which was why they never bothered to lock the door. If there were ever a fire, it wouldn't be much use if they couldn't get the door to the fire escape open! 'Well, we won't be getting any more visitors tonight, so let's all get back to bed and get some sleep.'

'This isn't funny any more,' said Sue, tight-lipped.

'Action Committee in the morning, yes, Rebecca?' said Elf determinedly.

Rebecca managed a wan smile.

'You bet,' she said.

'We'll *soon* solve the mystery,' vowed Margot.

Tish said nothing. She looked rather grim. Even the mention of their Action Committee didn't seem to please her very much.

TEN

GHOSTBUSTING

Mara was convinced that the legend must be true, that their floor at Court House was haunted by the ghost of a Victorian schoolmaster and his cat!

'Sarah Turner laughed at me when I scolded her!' she shuddered, as the Action Committee sat around talking the next morning. 'She said: "*Aaargh! What makes you think we made it up?*"'

'Oh, don't be daft, Mara,' said Tish.

It was Rebecca who remembered something vital; who hit on a possible explanation – one that could prove that the cat, at least, was certainly no ghost.

'Are you sure you just didn't have a really bad night-mare, Rebecca?' Elf was asking, as she munched her way through a bowl of muesli in the kitchen.

'What – and walked in my sleep and opened the fire escape door?' retorted Rebecca. She shook her head and sighed. 'It was a cat all right. I could feel its claws slightly, even through the duvet.'

'It was probably terrified, poor thing,' said Tish.

'Not as terrified as me.'

'Well, I still think it was a ghost cat,' said Mara stubbornly. 'Why has no one ever seen this wild cat, this stray? We asked everybody, didn't we, before? No one has ever seen it! And why should it choose to come to Court House, when it has the whole school to choose from?'

'Well, a stray like that would only come out at night,' said Elf sensibly. She was taking a tin of baked beans out of the cupboard. 'And maybe it just likes Court House. Maybe somebody's been putting food out for it. So do shut up, Mara, you're giving me the creeps.'

Rebecca stared at the tin of baked beans in Elf's hand. A picture of another tin flashed quite unexpectedly into her mind.

'The cylinder!' she gasped.

'Eh?' asked Tish.

'That tin you got out of the dustbin. It was an old *cat food* tin. But Mr and Mrs Barry haven't got a cat!'

'Lizzy Douglas!' exclaimed Sue. 'Let's go and see her. Quick!'

They charged all the way downstairs to the ground floor, knocked loudly, then burst into Lizzy Douglas's little single room. The window was closed and Lizzy was having a lie-in, reading in bed. And standing on her bedside locker –

A licked-out enamel dish.

'You little wretch!' exclaimed Rebecca, snatching the dish before the startled Lizzy could hide it. 'You've been putting cat food out at night, haven't you? Did you put some out last night?'

'What of it!' the Third Year girl blurted out, looking guilty. 'And you've no business barging into my room just because you're Fifth Years!'

'And you've no business trying to encourage your pet round here,' said Sue crisply. 'You know the rules. We'd all like to have our pets at school. Only then the place would be like a zoo!'

'Moggy gets hungry,' protested Lizzy, looking tearful. 'I'm not allowed to feed him in the daytime, am I, so I sometimes put a bit of food out for him at night when no one will see him. I don't even see him myself. He always comes when I'm asleep but I know he comes because the plate's always licked clean in the morning.'

'Except another cat's been eating it!' Rebecca told her. 'Not Moggy at all!'

'Who says?' she asked indignantly.

'*We* do,' replied Rebecca. She was already heading out of the room and the others followed. 'But there's nothing like finding out for sure!'

They raced across to Norris House and met Mrs Douglas in the hall. She was having a slight argument with a Third Year girl. 'Don't tell me there's no cotton wool in the box, Melissa, because I know there is – you obviously haven't looked properly. And since when have I allowed you to raid the first-aid box for art homework?'

'We've got to make a collage and I need it for the snow and the school shop's closed because it's Sunday!' protested the Third Year girl.

'Well, go and have another look then – and make sure you replace it later.' As the girl dashed off, Mrs Douglas turned to Rebecca and co.

'What an invasion! Can I help you, girls?'

Eagerly they questioned her.

'Moggy go out at night?' she laughed. 'Heavens, no. Come and have a look at him –'

She took them to the family flat and opened the door. There in the hall, in front of a log-burning stove, the large fluffy ginger and white lay snoring peacefully.

'He's getting old, too fat and lazy to go out. Too well fed, as well. That's where Moggy spends his nights.'

'But could Moggy have gone out *last* night?' insisted Rebecca.

'Never. He was in all night. What *is* all this about?'

'It's all right, Mrs Douglas!' Mara said quickly. Her brown eyes were shining with relief. This detective work had been fun! 'It's just that stray cat's been around again. The one we asked you about before. We just wondered if it could have been Moggy.'

'Oh, that's popped up again, has it?' she smiled.

They raced back and scolded Lizzy.

'You've been attracting some horrible old stray round here,' said Margot. 'That's what you've been doing!'

'And it really frightened Rebecca last night!'

'And I'm confiscating this plate,' said Rebecca, picking it up.

'Have you told on me?' asked Lizzy, white-faced.

'No,' said Rebecca. 'But if you ever put out a scrap more cat food on your window-sill at night, we'll report you to Mrs Barry and that's a promise.'

The six walked slowly back upstairs.

They were feeling subdued now, even Mara.

When they reached their floor they walked along to Rebecca's cubicle and went into a huddle there. Rebecca kicked off her shoes and threw herself on the bed.

'My arm's aching,' she said. 'Well,' she added heavily, 'that's solved the mystery of the cat, hasn't it?'

'But where does *that* leave us?' asked Sue, her brow deeply furrowed.

Margot picked up the big toy dog, idly. Elf looked at the chocolates.

'I won all that stuff at the disco,' said Rebecca, with a nod. 'Open one of the boxes, Elf. It'll help us to think.'

They munched away at the chocolates, thoughtfully.

'I'll tell you *exactly* where it leaves us,' said Tish, putting it into words at last. 'Somebody dressed up as "the schoolmaster" last night, the dear old ghost. Rebecca saw them when she came in. I *thought* you sounded a bit off when you said goodnight, Rebeck! Dressed up as a ghost to give Rebecca a fright. Waited till everyone was asleep and then let the cat in.'

'Worse than that,' said Elf unhappily. 'They didn't just let it in. They picked it up and *threw* it over into Rebecca's cubicle to give her the fright of her life.'

'Yes,' said Rebecca. 'It was chucked at me all right.'

'Who would do a thing like that?' asked Mara in distress. 'Oh, what a charming practical joke! Poor Rebecca.'

'Somebody's got a very peculiar sense of humour if you ask me,' said Elf, in deep puzzlement.

'Or else somebody's really got it in for me,' said Rebecca uneasily. She bit her lip. 'I think I'd almost rather have the ghost. I don't know which is worse.'

'What did the figure look like?' asked Tish, rather intensely. 'It couldn't possibly have been your friend Cliff?'

'Oh, no, Tish. No. He's a funster all right, but scaring

people's not his line, I'm quite sure. Besides, I saw him go off. And where would he have got that gown from or whatever it was? And besides *again*, Cliff's short –'

'Was the person tall, then?' asked Tish quickly. 'The person who brought the cat in with them?'

'Yes. About as tall as . . . well, Robbie,' Rebecca said, 'but I've just realized something. They didn't bring the cat *in* with them. The cat was on the roof. I saw its eyes! It was peering in through the skylight when the person was already in here.'

'What would the cat be on the roof for?' asked Mara inconsequentially.

'Looking for birds, I expect,' said Margot.

But Tish was walking out of the cubicle, followed by Sue. She sounded impatient.

'Come on, you lot, Rebecca can rest for a bit. We've got to find out who this joker is – we'd better start looking for clues. The sooner the better.'

She seemed to be rather on edge.

As Rebecca lolled on her bed, back resting against the pillows, deep in thought, Aba stopped by to say hello.

'Hiya,' said the Nigerian girl, looking pleased. 'I've just had a peep at Tish's coursework. I make all my answers the same as hers so I guess I'm doing all right! Now I can go and have a swim with a clear conscience.'

'I must have a look myself later on,' remembered Rebecca, 'and try and find out about vectors. Has to be in tomorrow, doesn't it.'

'What's all the excitement about, anyway?' asked Aba, nodding in the direction of the fire escape. Rebecca's five friends were out there, swarming up and down the metal treads, hunting around on the ground as well. 'What's going on?'

'Just ghostbusting,' said Rebecca.

'Ghostbusting?'

'Looking for clues,' said Rebecca wearily. She played the whole thing down. 'Some silly fool's latched on to that ghost business. Played a trick last night. Let that stray cat in. Didn't you hear me scream? Anyway, they want to find out who.'

'You not helping?' smiled Aba, as she left.

'No, I'm just trying to think,' replied Rebecca.

She'd been thinking hard.

Sue came to see her soon after, waving a narrow ribbon of blue streamer.

'This anything, Rebeck?'

'Afraid not. That was in my hair last night, from the disco. Sue —'

Rebecca looked around to make sure they were alone, and then whispered:

'Tish is wondering if it could have been Robbie, isn't she?'

Sue looked down at the floor, silent, lips pursed — and Rebecca knew that she'd guessed correctly.

'Well, what do you think, Sue?'

Sue shrugged.

'How was the Garth disco, anyway?' Rebecca persisted. 'Did Robbie show up?'

'For about five minutes, that's all. He's not on good form lately, is he? Justy says he's working too hard. And he's fed up about his car being finished. And he's fed up about your arm —'

'– and about me going to the disco with Cliff?' questioned Rebecca.

'Yes, Justy said he was jealous,' admitted Sue, doubtfully. 'And he *does* know about the ghost business and about your seeing the cat . . .'

'So what's the verdict, Sue?'

'I'd say it was pretty unbelievable.'

Rebecca sighed with relief.

'Exactly. So would I,' said Rebecca, with an unpleasant feeling in the pit of her stomach at the very thought of it. 'So just tell Tish that from me, would you –?'

She broke off as Elf suddenly appeared, waving her arms excitedly.

'Quick, Sue! Margot's found something, we think it's a clue. On the fire escape! And along the garden path as well. Quick –'

They raced off. Rebecca leapt off her bed.

'Wait for me!' she cried. She fumbled to find her shoes, which had disappeared under the bed somewhere. Oh, blow her shoes!

She ran out of her cubicle barefoot and rushed out on to the balcony to see what was happening.

ELEVEN

CULPRIT NUMBER ONE...

'What is it? What have you found?' Rebecca called down. They were near the bottom of the fire escape, huddled round one of the metal treads. Sue had gone down on one knee, to examine it. 'Let me see!'

She descended the clanking staircase.

'It's tiny drops of blood, Rebeck!' announced Sue. She pointed towards the tread. 'Look!'

Screwing up her nose, Rebecca pushed closer and looked. Sure enough, there were spots on the step that looked like blood! 'Ugh!' she said.

Margot stood at the foot of the fire escape, pointing down the garden. A little white path wound its way through the garden, past Mrs Barrington's washing line and clothes prop, to the gate at the end.

'There's more down there, along the path!' Margot explained to Rebecca. 'Just some tiny drops, near Mrs Barry's washing line.'

'Blood!' exclaimed Rebecca. She sat down on one of the steps. 'Of *course*!'

'Of course what?' demanded Tish urgently.

They all gathered round.

'That cry I heard last night!' Rebecca realized. 'An awful cry of pain – just before the cat yowled like a banshee and came sailing over the top of my cubie –' She clapped her hands in realization. 'The cat attacked them. Must have done! That was why they cried out. They'd been scratched!'

'Really torn, I should think!' said Elf, shuddering as she looked at the tiny drops of blood. 'They'll have an awful deep scratch by the look of this. Serves them right!'

'We must get on the trail!' said Mara. 'Where does the path lead? After it goes through the gate?'

'Across to the trees,' said Sue. 'Where Rebecca saw the joker standing in the first place. They obviously just headed back the way they'd come.'

'Anyway,' said Margot practically, 'the trail peters out by Mrs Barry's washing line. They must have stopped bleeding by then.'

'Just as well or they'd need a blood transfusion by this morning!' exclaimed Elf. Tish just looked glum and remained silent.

'The *real* clue,' Rebecca was saying thoughtfully, 'is our ghost'll have a livid scratch on their hands or arms or somewhere, not very easy to hide, that.'

'Sue, go and ring Justy!' Tish suddenly blurted out. 'Ring him and ask him if –'

'I *certainly will not*!' flared Sue, her eyes glittering like daggers at Tish from behind her spectacles. 'He'd think I'd gone mad.'

The other three stared at them in surprise – what was all this about? But Rebecca's thoughts were racing. Robbie wouldn't have played that horrible trick. Robbie wouldn't be the person with the scratch. She'd never ever believe that. But who – who –?

'The path doesn't lead straight to the trees,' she said, thinking out loud. 'It goes past Norris House first . . .'

There was something bothering her, something she'd heard that seemed to connect with this, but she couldn't quite place it. Mara got there first.

'The cotton wool!' she cried. 'Remember? The cotton wool was missing from the first-aid box, that was what Melissa Parker said!'

'Good point, Mara,' said Elf. 'I wonder if there could be anything in that.'

'Let's find out!' exclaimed Tish. She jumped down the last three steps of the fire escape, suddenly exuberant again. 'Let's go over to Norris and see who pinched it – and why!'

'Wait for me, I'll get my shoes!' cried Rebecca, hurtling back up the fire escape. 'I'm coming with you!'

But led by Tish the others were already charging down the garden path on their way to Norris.

By the time Rebecca got over to the neighbouring boarding house and investigated the hall, they'd vanished. A group of Third Year girls was gathered round the first-aid box, which was kept under the stairs, chattering excitedly. Amongst them was Melissa Parker.

'Where've they gone?' asked Rebecca. 'The others?'

'Have you come about the cotton wool, too? Somebody *did* filch it from the box!' said Melissa, full of importance. 'So I was right. And when they came and put it back, they'd nearly used it all and there wasn't enough left for my collage . . .'

'Who came and put it back?' Rebecca interrupted impatiently. 'And where've my friends gone?'

'That room along there,' said another girl, pointing down the corridor. 'The one at the end.'

'Thanks!' jerked Rebecca and rushed off.

'What's this all about anyway?' Melissa called out.

But Rebecca had already reached the room at the end of the corridor. The door was ajar. She could hear Tish's raised voice – and Mara's.

Slowly she pushed open the door.

The occupant of the room sat at her work table, which was covered in school books, half-completed maths coursework and various piles of paper. The others were all gathered round her, angry, accusing. A wodge of cotton wool lay on the window-sill, next to a bottle of iodine. Rebecca's eyes went straight to the back of the girl's hand, which was stained with iodine.

On the back of the hand were two livid scratches.

'You!' said Rebecca, stunned. 'You!'

It was a red-faced and miserable Roberta Jones.

'Look at this, Rebecca!' cried Mara. She was waving some sheets of paper. 'Photocopies! That's what she was doing last night! She crept in and copied Tish's coursework on my new machine! She was going to put all Tish's answers in her own booklet.'

That odd little swishing sound Rebecca had heard last night. It had been the photocopy machine!

'Stupid, isn't it?' snorted Tish. But she looked almost relieved.

Rebecca's mouth opened and then closed again.

'Honestly, Bert. Sneaking around our floor at night!'

said Margot angrily. 'Throwing that cat at Rebecca and giving her the fright of her life, just to save yourself from being found out!'

'I didn't mean to give Rebecca a fright!' protested the large girl, tears brimming up in her eyes. 'I just happened to see the cat on my way out. Then I thought if I picked it up and put it on the big table next to the copy machine, you'd all think it was the cat you'd heard making a noise!'

'Then what happened?' asked Rebecca, at last finding her voice.

'When I picked it up, it was wild – savage! Its claws went right into my skin – look!' She held up her hand. 'I was terrified – I thought it'd go for my face as well. So I just hurled it high in the air, to get it away from me! I didn't mean it to go over the top of your cubie, Rebecca!' She turned to her, pleadingly. 'I never meant to give you a fright! I never even thought about that ghost business. That was only a joke or something, wasn't it? It never entered my head –'

They were all silent for a moment, digesting this. Then –

'Rubbish!' exploded Sue. 'Never entered your head? You dressed up as the ghost before you came in!'

'I – I – did not –' protested Roberta.

'Yes, you did. *Rebecca saw you.* Earlier! Was that a precaution? In case any of us woke up while you were using the copier? To make sure none of us would recognize you? Just be frightened out of our wits instead?'

'Stop it!' gasped Roberta. 'What on earth are you talking about?'

'You know perfectly well what Sue's talking about,

Robert,' said Tish angrily. 'OK, so you were desperate about your maths – but to plan it all so carefully! With such cunning. Quite happy to scare people rather than be found out. You always did like dressing up! Where did you get the schoolmaster's gown from?'

'Schoolmaster's gown –?' frowned Roberta.

'Yes,' chimed in Margot. 'And –'

But Rebecca cut her short.

'Hadn't we better give Roberta a chance to speak?' she asked quietly.

'Thank you!' said Roberta. She was looking very indignant now. She took a deep breath. 'I don't know what you're talking about. What gown?' She looked straight at Tish. 'I did *not* plan everything out carefully. That's the last thing I did! I sat here in my room till gone midnight last night, getting more and more depressed about my maths. I just decided on the spur of the moment! I got my mini-torch and sneaked across to your fire escape in my pyjamas. I guessed the door might be open. I knew Tish would just have left her coursework lying on the big table for everyone to look at if they wanted to! I crept up one lunch hour and looked at the last lot when I was stuck! So I didn't see what harm . . .'

Tish looked disconcerted. It was obvious that Roberta was telling the truth. She glanced at Rebecca.

'Well, you saw the "ghost", Rebeck. What do *you* think?'

Roberta Jones scraped her chair back and stood up and faced Rebecca.

'Well. Was it me or wasn't it?'

Rebecca looked her up and down. Although Roberta was tall and her face quite boyish looking if she tied her hair back, Rebecca was quite sure about it. She had been for some minutes.

'No,' she sighed. 'It wasn't you, Robert. It definitely was not *you* over by the sycamore trees. It must have been somebody else.'

'Thank you,' replied the other girl, with as much dignity as she could muster. She sat down again.

They all fell silent. A cloud crossed Tish's face.

She rummaged round on Roberta's table and collected up all the photocopied sheets, one by one. It covered most of her maths coursework.

'Well, I wouldn't waste your time with these, if I were you,' she said bad-temperedly. 'We're going back to Court now. I'll take these back with me if you *don't* mind. What a stupid waste of time! You could have asked me for some help, couldn't you? Just copying out my work parrot-fashion would be really asking for trouble. You'd have looked such a fool when you had your oral! Miss Holt would have been furious! She'd have ended up not giving you any grade at all!'

'I've already realized that,' said Roberta miserably, 'now I've had a good look at it. That's why I haven't copied anything in.'

She stared sullenly at the stinging scratches on the back of her hand.

'Anyway – I don't want to be a vet any more, so what does it matter.'

'Thank goodness for that,' said Sue drily, as they all marched out of the room.

TWELVE

...AND CULPRIT NUMBER TWO

So who was the ghost? Who was the person that Rebecca had seen? It hung like a shadow over the morning. And Tish wasn't much help, either.

'My brother's a real embarrassment to me, that's all I can say. I'd stick with Cliff, if I were you, Rebeck.'

They'd all gone for a swim except Rebecca and now they were back, drinking tea on the balcony, discussing things. There was a watery autumn sun. The leaves were fluttering off the sycamore trees, just beyond Norris there. Tish was convinced that the person Rebecca had seen there in the moonlight, so briefly, must have been Robbie. Spying on her, because she'd been to the disco with Cliff.

'What – dressed up as a ghost?' Rebecca said scornfully. 'Don't be silly.'

'Oh, no, not that!' replied Tish. 'You must have made a mistake about that. I expect he had his coat flung over his shoulders, just loose. The way he does. You said you only caught a glimpse.'

'Yes,' said Rebecca. It was true that Robbie often slung

his coat round his shoulders, rather than put it on properly. Was that what he'd done? Walked morosely through the night from Garth College, his coat slung round his shoulders to keep the rain off. Decided to get a look at Cliff perhaps? The very thought made her furious. But when she closed her eyes and pictured in her mind the mysterious figure she'd seen, it didn't seem right. 'No, Tish,' she said. 'I don't think it was Robbie. It better not have been.'

'He has been working pretty hard,' pondered Sue, uneasily. 'Maybe getting moody about things. You know how Justy was, last term.'

Sue had never even entertained the trick idea. But this was looking slightly more believable.

'That is not a good excuse!' said Mara firmly. 'Jealousy is a very bad thing. And, in any case, he would have a nerve. Remember Ingrid!'

'Am I ever likely to forget her?' said Rebecca, with a rueful smile. And she thought: Robbie jealous? Spying on me? Yes, that certainly would be a nerve. But I can't believe it . . . I won't. I won't think about it any more.

Aloud, she said:

'Tish, you wouldn't like to explain vectors to me, would you? I oughtn't to need it but I do.'

'Me, too!' said Mara eagerly.

'And I must do some violin practice,' said Sue guiltily.

'And you promised to test my French vocab, Elf!' said Margot.

Rebecca and Mara sat with Tish at the big table for almost an hour. She got out pencil and paper and explained the mysteries of vectors to them. She even set some problems for them which they got right.

'It's obvious now,' laughed Rebecca in relief, when they'd finished. It had been very nearly enjoyable: and at least it had helped her banish those dark thoughts about Robbie to the back of her mind.

'We should have got Robert the Robot over here,' said Tish suddenly.

'Robert?' asked Mara in horror. 'You are joking, Ishbel Anderson.'

'Am I?' said Tish thoughtfully. She looked unhappy. 'Poor Robert. Such a pointless expedition. She must have been desperate. Coming over here in the middle of the night like that! I ticked her off earlier, I said: "You could have asked me for some help, couldn't you?" *But she did!* She kept asking for help. And nobody wanted to know. The Nathan twins. Debbie Rickard, especially not her. Nor Joss, what's the betting. Me. None of us. How unfair it must have looked! Don't you see – we drove her to it in the end?'

Rebecca and Mara fell silent and exchanged uncomfortable looks.

There was quite a lot of truth in what Tish was saying.

But Rebecca forgot about Roberta and soon started thinking about Robbie again. As she washed her face and hands before lunch, awkwardly, trying not to splash the bandage on her bad arm, the little cloud settled over her once more. Could it possibly have been Robbie, spying on her?

Even as she dismissed the thought, wearily, it reminded her that the barrier between them created by the car accident continued to make mischief. Before that, she wouldn't have listened to Tish's ravings even for a moment. Drat this bandage, now she'd got it wet after all! Oh, it would have been nice to have had a swim this morning!

And anyway, when was she going to play some tennis matches again – proper matches? And some hockey! The doctor was still telling her she had to be careful. It seemed to be dragging on for years! It was all Robbie's fault!

They all trooped downstairs to go across to the dining hall for Sunday lunch. When they reached the ground floor, the phone rang. 'It's for you, Rebecca!' shouted Lucy Hubbard.

Rebecca took the phone and told the others she'd see them in hall '*Save me plenty of roast! Hello – who is it?*'

'Rebecca!'

'Cliff!' she said, with pleasure. 'Is your brother OK? Did anything happen to him? Is everything all right?'

'Tell you in a minute!' said Cliff, keeping his voice low. 'But first – how about you? D'you get into trouble for being late?'

'No!' giggled Rebecca. It was her turn to lower her voice. 'The others covered up for me. But what about Tom? Is he all right?'

'He's all right *now*!' Cliff whispered. 'He was fuming last night! Flaming mad with me! You see –'

'What?'

'His car wouldn't start – the rain, I suppose. That put him in a bad temper for a start! So he phoned a minicab. Told it to go and pick us up from the High, take you back, then bring me home to our address and he'd settle up.'

'Oh, no,' groaned Rebecca.

'So of course the minicab turned up at our house,

empty. The driver was stroppy about not being able to find us and charged Tom extra. Tom was left sitting at home worrying what to do, and so he hopped on his bike and pedalled over to Trebizon to see if there was any sign of us. He pedalled round the grounds getting madder and madder in a dripping wet cycle cape –'

'*Cycle cape?*' exclaimed Rebecca.

'Yes, what's so thrilling about that? And then he spotted you! Up on your balcony after I'd gone. A girl cavorting around in disco clothes, he told me, chucking things over the side as though she hadn't a care in the world!'

Rebecca laughed out loud in sheer relief – and amazement.

The magisterial figure! Cliff's brother, Tom. Standing there behind the trees in his cycle cape, feeling furious after all the worry he'd been through!

'Then he saw me and gave me a rocket!' Cliff was saying. 'But at least I got a lift home on his crossbar. What's so funny, Rebecca?'

'Oh, Cliff, it's not a bit funny,' she said hastily. 'It's awful. Weren't we thoughtless? We should have *waited*. It was all my fault for panicking. Listen, Cliff, the least I can do is pay for the minicab.'

'It was my idea to get the lift in the van, wasn't it?' said Cliff cheerfully. 'I've paid Tom, don't worry. You can buy me a coffee some time.'

He chortled quietly into the phone then.

'But didn't we have a great time? Wasn't it a great disco, Rebecca?'

'Just about the best, Cliff!'

She ran all the way to the dining hall, her feet scuffling

joyfully through fallen leaves. The others had already started eating. Sunday lunch – her favourite meal! The roast potatoes looked delicious.

'You're looking cheerful!' said Mara, as she squeezed into her chair.

'I'm feeling it,' replied Rebecca. She leaned forward and whispered to them, laughing: 'I've found out who the so-called ghost was last night. The mystery figure by the trees.'

'Who? Who?' they all cried.

She turned to Tish.

'You should have more faith in your brother, Tish! It wasn't *your* brother at all. It was Cliff's.'

The same afternoon, searching for her tennis ball round the back of Norris House, Rebecca glanced through a window and espied Tish and Roberta with their heads together at the work table in Roberta's room.

'I was just helping her a bit!' said Tish defensively, when Rebecca mentioned it later. 'She's not that bad. She's decided to give up the idea of the top papers now. But there's no reason why she shouldn't get a C if she keeps her head and learns a few theorems properly. She's going to ask if she can go back down to Div 3. She's already phoned her father and told him.'

'Poor Mr Jones must be getting a bit confused,' smiled Rebecca, thinking how much she liked the Anderson family.

THIRTEEN

SHADOWS LIFTED

The ghosts had been laid: the shadows lifted. Thereafter life on the top floor of Court House continued as sweet and sunlit and unghostly as Rebecca had always imagined it would be. The nocturnal visitor which had been driven by hunger into Trebizon school's heartland and then found food so thoughtfully put out at nights, ceased to visit once the supplies dried up. But somebody actually saw the semi-wild cat one day in broad daylight, on the far side of the parkland where the deer grazed, with a small rabbit in its mouth.

The Fifth Years all handed in their maths course-work, 'the extended set task', on time and over the next fortnight the work was duly marked and each girl tested orally by a member of Trebizon's maths staff.

When the grades were announced, Roberta had managed to scrape a creditable C, without cheating this time. Mara got a B and so did Rebecca – she narrowly missed getting an A! Debbie Rickard on the other hand, who'd been expected to get an A, had to be given a B – and Miss

Gates summonsed her parents to school for the inevitable showdown.

'We're all very concerned,' the senior mistress told them. 'You're giving Deborah far too much help with her GCSE coursework. Several members of staff have detected it. You're not doing her any favours as must be obvious from her grades this term. She's a capable girl – clever, in fact. You should have more faith in your daughter.'

Mr and Mrs Rickard looked chastened. Painfully they'd been coming to certain conclusions themselves, prompted by quarrels at home which usually ended with Debbie flouncing upstairs and slamming her bedroom door.

'We feel we've made a mistake,' said Debbie's father.

'She's not happy as a day girl. She seems to be missing her friends,' explained her mother. 'We feel that may be why her work's gone downhill. Nothing to do with us, of course,' she added hastily. 'Would it be possible for her to start boarding again next term?'

'Yes, why not?' replied Miss Gates, in relief.

And decided to leave it at that.

Robbie Anderson's work wasn't going downhill, far from it. After he'd written his Oxford entrance-exam papers at Garth College, he telephoned Rebecca in a state of euphoria.

'I know I've done brilliantly in the maths papers – and OK in the physics as well!' he exclaimed. 'All the things I've worked on came up and I've checked some of the tough ones with my tutors and apparently I got them right!'

'Oh Robbie, that's wonderful,' said Rebecca, admiringly. 'And what about the General Paper?'

'Oh, I fudged some essays together for that all right,' he said, still sounding carefree.

'What happens next?'

'Well, assuming I've passed and I'm sure I *have*, I'll go up to Oxford in two weeks' time and stay at the college and have interviews! That's the final hurdle – the interviews.'

Rebecca smiled. It was nice to hear Robbie sounding so confident.

To her distinct satisfaction, she was forging ahead on all fronts with her own school work. She'd now decided to set her sights on getting all A and B grades in GCSE next summer! If she could achieve that, then even more good would have come of the stupid car accident than she'd vowed at the time! That would please Dad, wouldn't it?

Her wrist and arm were almost better. Very soon now she'd be playing tennis again. Both Joss Vining and Alison Hissup, who was this year's Head of Games, had promised her singles. And with luck she'd fit in a training session with the county squad at Exonford before the end of term.

In the meantime, it had been surprisingly pleasant to find herself getting good at table tennis – though not as good as Elf or Margot – and finding time to go to cookery club and even fit in some dancing classes. And she was doing brilliantly at Latin. Mr Pargiter was giving her bits of Tacitus to translate to 'stretch' her (it was really Sixth Form work) and that passage of Nero and Agrippina had been pounced on by Suky Morris for the *Trebizon*

Journal! A really good translation, she'd said, it could go on the new 'merit' pages.

It was Justin Thomas who struck a slightly sour note about Robbie's Oxford hopes. Both boys were called up for interviews at their respective colleges. They returned to the west country on the Friday and Rebecca and Sue met them in Fenners on the Saturday afternoon.

Justin was his usual quiet self but Robbie was in a state of great excitement, full of the trip to Oxford, the ancient college he'd stayed at and everything that had taken place there. As Rebecca poured out tea for the four of them, he talked non-stop.

'The philosophy interview was weird!' he announced with a grin. 'Some really odd questions. Listen to this one. A man went into the desert and he had two enemies. One filled his water bottle with poison and the other shot a hole in it, so that it ran out. He died of thirst, so which one killed him?'

Rebecca and Sue discussed this problem with great animation.

'Well, in a way neither of them killed him because he died of thirst – he died of natural causes.'

'No, that can't be right, Sue, because if there'd been water in his bottle he wouldn't have died. So the one who put the poison in . . .'

'No, the one who shot the hole in the bottle. He thought there was water in it and so it was he who performed the final, murderous act –'

'No, he didn't! You could argue that *he* saved the man's life. If he hadn't shot a hole in that water bottle, the man would have drunk the poison . . .'

'But the man died anyway.'

And so on. For several minutes.

Robbie and Justin listened to the girls in amusement. Finally, when the discussion petered out, Justy turned to Robbie and said:

'Well, did you say all that at the interview?'

'No fear,' said Robbie. 'I just said the question was unanswerable.'

'But didn't you philosophize about it a bit?' asked Justy.

'Nope,' said Robbie, stabbing a cream cake with a fork. He exuded confidence. 'I prefer questions that have a cut and dried answer. I got on really well with the economics don!'

Justy looked nonplussed and Rebecca noted that a slight furrow crossed his brow.

'Hope you've chosen the right course, Rob,' he muttered under his breath. But Robbie had already changed the subject and was asking Rebecca about her tennis. How had her games of singles gone?

It was December now but the days were still mild. Rebecca's injury had been pronounced completely cured at last. While Robbie had been up in Oxford, she'd played her first hard tennis again. Proper singles matches, first against Joss and then against Alison. She'd been soundly beaten in both cases, which was rather alarming.

'But only to be expected,' she explained ruefully. 'I'm so rusty! I'm going to Exonford tomorrow – county squad training. Mrs Ericson says I'm certain to be badly in need of it!'

Robbie was crestfallen at her news.

'Don't worry, Robbie!' Rebecca exclaimed. She looked very determined. 'I'll come back!'

*

By the last week of term, the Oxford results were coming in. On the Monday morning, Miss Welbeck announced in assembly that both Suky Morris and Sujata Seal had been offered places. More girls had applied to Cambridge this year – their results would come later.

Justin Thomas had got into Oxford! His college admissions tutor had telephoned the school. Three or four other boys had been phoned as well.

'Has Robbie had any news?' asked Rebecca anxiously.

'Not yet,' replied Sue. 'I expect he'll hear soon!'

But by Wednesday night, Robbie still hadn't heard anything.

'I don't think I've got in, Rebeck,' he said to her on the phone. She'd never heard him so subdued. 'That's what it looks like.'

'Oh, Robbie, surely not.'

'They ring, if they want you! They ring pretty quickly. That's what I've heard, anyway. It's looking bad, isn't it? I can't stand the suspense any longer. I'm going to go and see Doctor Simpson in the morning and ask him if he can ring them up! Find out what's happening!'

'Surely it'll be all right, Robbie,' said Rebecca, feeling upset.

But it wasn't all right.

He came to see her after school on Thursday, bringing her Christmas present. All the others had gone carol singing, but Rebecca had stayed back to see Robbie. They sat outside together, half-way down the fire escape. Robbie was fighting back the tears.

In spite of alphas for his maths and physics papers, he'd failed the General Paper. Following his interviews, the college had decided with great regret that in view of the stiff competition for places on the PPE course, they couldn't offer him one. A letter was in the post.

'Poor Robbie!' said Rebecca, in dismay. 'After all your hard work. It's not fair!'

They sat there for a while and then Robbie said:

'It was perfectly fair. I wasn't interested in politics and philosophy and they saw it straight away. I didn't know what course I wanted to do when I filled up the form – I still don't. I just made something up.'

Like Roberta! thought Rebecca.

They walked across to main school together, along the lamplit footpaths. Rebecca badly needed to spend some time in the library if she were to finish her history coursework before they broke up next day for Christmas.

Outside the eighteenth-century building they stood in a pool of light cast by the great windows of the old library. The figure of Suky Morris drifted past, inside, a pile of books in her arms.

Robbie stood and gazed at Rebecca, gently lifting her left arm and then letting it drop again. 'Is it really better?' he asked.

'Yes.'

'Dull, but useful,' mused Robbie.

'What is? Who is?'

'Doctors.'

Rebecca smiled in surprise, flexed her muscles and clenched her fist in the air. 'Look! Stronger than the other one now!'

'What a term! The way that deer just appeared from nowhere!' sighed Robbie. 'The whole thing shook you up quite badly, didn't it? Imagining ghosts, even. That's not like you to be nervous, Rebeck!' He knew all about it now.

'And I blame myself, whatever you say about the seat belt. I was bowling along too fast, wasn't I? Come on, admit it.'

Rebecca gazed at him. There was a moist patch on one of his cheeks.

'Maybe,' she said. 'Maybe a teeny bit fast.'

She dried his moist cheek with a clean handkerchief and kissed it dry as well.

'Except it doesn't matter any more, Robbie.'

It was lovely to be able to say that – and mean it. The last shadow had been lifted.

School broke up and Rebecca sat back in the long-distance coach to her grandmother's, feeling luxurious, going through the little presents from her friends and all her Christmas cards.

There were some extra ones this year. A really nice card from Roberta Jones – and one with a kitten peering out of a Christmas stocking from Lizzy Douglas. Her last glimpse of Lizzy was of her outside Norris with Moggy in her arms. She'd be spending three whole weeks with her parents now, and be able to feed and cuddle her pet to her heart's content. There's no day without night, thought Rebecca. *No happiness without suffering!*

Cliff had sent her a scarf. It was such fun to have met up with Cliff Haynes again! Robbie had smiled at her and said: 'I'm not going to ask you not to see Cliff next term, though I'd like to.' And she'd replied firmly: 'Well, that's just as well then, isn't it?'

Mr Pargiter had given her a Christmas card: all the members of the Latin group had got one. It was a small group and they'd had a lot of fun with Pargie, as they called him. But Rebecca's card included congratulations (in Latin of course!) for what he described as remarkable progress this term.

Staring at it, she was reminded that her school report would soon be on its way to her parents. What would it say? And come to think of it, what did her last report say, the one that Mum and Dad were so secretive about? When were they going to tell her what was in it? The letters had been coming steadily from Saudi Arabia this term, but still no mention of that.

Robbie's Christmas present was a box of best, top-quality tennis balls. He'd scribbled in felt tip on the outside of the box: *Rebecca Mason will be back!*

And you'll be back, too, Robbie, thought Rebecca, a lump coming to her throat as she looked at the message. That's what his headmaster Doctor Simpson had told him. He'd made a bad blunder and chosen the wrong course, against the school's advice, too. They must wait and see exactly what the letter from Oxford had to say. But he'd be back. Once he'd sorted himself out.

Would *she*? The training session at Exonford hadn't been much good but Mrs Ericson had told her she had to be patient! Would she climb back? How long was it going to take?

Anyhow, the Trebizon film was going to be shown on TV at last!

It was going out on Boxing Day – millions of people would see it! They'd see her playing the best four tennis games of her life. Tucking into turkey sandwiches and Gran's mince pies, she'd sit glued to the television and re-live that Fourth Year triumph. Who else would see it? Anyone exciting?

And she and Gran would video the film and have a

permanent record: Mum and Dad would see it when they came home on leave next summer.

She decided, dozily, as the coach slid along the M 5 in a fast lane, that the man in the desert had been killed by the one who shot a hole in the water bottle. After all, that deprived him of anything to drink and he died of thirst, didn't he?

If the other one had killed him, he'd have died of poisoning, wouldn't he?